Baking for Keeps

Baking for Keeps

A Bachelor Bake-Off Romance

Jessica Gilmore

TULE
PUBLISHING

Baking for Keeps
Copyright © 2017 Jessica Gilmore
Tule Publishing First Printing, March 2017

The Tule Publishing Group, LLC

ISBN: 978-1-946772-21-3

Dedication

For Dan and Abby, much love and grateful thanks as always for your patience and the endless cups of tea xxx

Dear Reader

For the last couple of years I have loved visiting Marietta as a reader. Mountains, lakes and a gorgeous small town full of cowboys and the women who tame them – what's not to love? So you can imagine how thrilled I was when I was asked to contribute my own story to the Marietta community! I was even more thrilled to discover I would be setting my story during a Bachelor Bake-Off competition, working with talented authors like Shirley, Kate, Jennifer and Lara. Collaborating on the Bake-Off has been an absolute joy – and bringing my small-town-loving heroine, Lacey, and aloof city boy Zac to life even more so, not to mention Lacey's wonderful great aunts and their home, Crooked Corner, where you'll always be welcomed with a hot cup of coffee and a delicious slice of cake. I do hope you enjoy reading Lacey and Zac's story as much as I enjoyed writing it.

Love Jessica

Chapter One

"THIS IS LACEY Hathaway and you're listening to drive time here on KMCM, Paradise Valley's very own radio station. I hope everyone's enjoying this glorious sunny January day. Later on today we'll be chatting to Lisa Renee about winter celebrity weddings and Nell will be popping in to answer your questions on how to deal with hat hair, so get texting and calling. I'll even respond to the odd tweet!

"Just a reminder it's cold out there, folks, and the roads are *iiiicyyyy*! Watch yourselves on the drive home, it doesn't matter if it takes a little longer, I'm here keeping you company through till six. Now I don't know about you guys but when the snow's on the ground and the mercury's dropped, I'm like a bear fattening up for hibernation. I want baked goods and plenty of them, give me cake and pie and cookies until I burst! Well, my luck is in because we're just two weeks away from Marietta's first Bachelor Bake-Off and there are going to be plenty of tasty treats in the kitchen. Insert your own pun here, ladies!"

Zac Malone sighed and hit the button on the car radio.

The only thing he disliked more than small towns was small-town radio, especially chipper small-town radio hosts who rabbited on about small-town concerns. He searched for the nearest public radio station and cursed under his breath as a stream of static hissed out of the speakers. Looked like it was Miss Chipper or nothing. Luckily he was a man who didn't mind the sound of his own thoughts.

The radio host had been right about one thing: it *was* icy out despite the winter blue skies and the pale sliver of sun low in the sky. Snow coated the mountains all around him and dusted the windy mountain road, hiding the worst of the patches of black ice and making the driving treacherous going. Zac checked his GPS. Not far now, luckily; the sun was beginning to drop behind the mountains and he didn't much fancy being out on these unknown roads on a late January night. He hit dial on his hands-free, tapping the steering wheel impatiently until his PA's voice rang out. "Hi there, Zac."

"Katie," he acknowledged more curtly than he intended. Her naturally flirty manner always made him tense up. He sensed that she was fully aware of that fact and ramped up her manner accordingly.

Sure enough her voice dropped suggestively. "How's cowboy country? Make sure you send us some pictures if you go native. I bet you look good on a horse."

Zac ignored her second comment. "So far Montana is covered in snow and ridiculously cold." He didn't usually venture this far north. Luckily the car he'd rented at the airport was fully equipped with winter tires, a shovel, and a blanket. If he didn't reach his destination soon he had an inkling he might need them. "You haven't sent me the coordinates yet. Where's the motel?"

"Ah, about that…"

"Yes?"

"There isn't actually a motel in town. Marietta isn't big on chains. And the main hotel is a little over budget for a long stay, and booked out at the weekends anyway for weddings and all…" Katie finally stopped for breath.

"So?"

"So you're booked in at an adorable-sounding guest-house. The Crooked Corner—isn't that the quaintest thing you ever heard?"

Zac's jaw set. Quaint was another thing on the list of things he didn't do. "A guesthouse?" He wasn't a fussy guy. He just insisted that Katie book him into a nice anonymous motel somewhere. The kind where people minded their own business and nobody made small talk over coffee. Or, indeed, at any time. "Katie…"

"Zac, there's nowhere else in town," she said hurriedly. "It's all B&Bs and guesthouses and inns. Tourist-friendly place, you know? And, with the weather and all, I didn't think you would want to be in the next town over. This place isn't a full-time guesthouse, the owners have a suite of rooms they let out every now and then on a medium-term basis. It comes with breakfast and dinner but there are no other guests. It's more like lodging than anything else. It's run by two sisters-in-law, Priscilla and Patty Hathaway—according to their website everyone calls them Aunt Patty and Aunt Priscilla. How cute do they sound?"

Cute was the last thing he wanted in a temporary home and he certainly didn't need two pseudo aunts fussing over him. Zac drummed his fingers harder on the wheel. This was far from ideal—but then everything about this assignment was wrong. An audit, training, and consultancy all in one package meant an extended stay of possibly a couple of months.

Normally he specialized in quick jobs in the southwest of the country, preferring to work in cities wherever possible, but one of his most trusted employees was ill and there was no one else free at short notice Zac could rely on to cover such an important job. So here he was, far out of his comfort zone. And now he had nowhere suitable to stay. He'd just have to work harder than ever so he could get out as fast as he could. "Fine. Send me the coordinates."

It only took another quarter of an hour to reach Crooked Corner. That was plenty long enough for Zac to realize that Marietta was everything he'd been dreading it would be; a small town, all chocolate box storefronts and rosy-cheeked children playing in the snow. The kind of place where everyone knew everyone else's name and everyone else's business. The kind of place he'd spent his entire adult life escaping from.

He slowed down as a teen boy mooched past, his thin jacket inadequate against the cold, his face set with a weary determination that Zac recognized all too well. "Dammit," he said softly. He'd spent far too long burying his demons to let this one-horse town dig them up again.

He turned his attention back to his route, following the GPS down Bramble Lane, his eyes skimming indifferently over the old mansions lining the road until the anonymous voice told him to pull in at a large Victorian house, all interesting angles and turrets, on the corner of Bramble Lane and 2nd Avenue. Painted white with a red trim, wide steps led up to a wraparound porch, several bird feeders hanging from the rail. The front door was also a cherry red, the rocker next to it painted the same color and heaped with bright cushions. He should've brought his sunglasses.

Zac decided to leave his bags in the car until he'd seen his rooms. Any sign of communal living space or a repeat of that glossy red in his rooms and he was heading to the nearest motel, wintry roads or not. He made his way to the porch steps, feet slipping a little on the packed snow. He was going to need winter boots. And—he shivered as a chill wind whistled past and through him—a thicker coat. His mind flew to the boy he'd seen just a few moments earlier. Did he have a thick coat at home he'd refused to wear with a teen's disdain or was he doing the best with what little he had?

"Zac Malone? Come in, come in!" Zac blinked in surprise as the red door was flung open and a tall figure stood beaming at him. "I'm Patty Hathaway but everyone calls me Aunt Patty and you must absolutely do the same. Is that the only coat you have? We'll need to send you over to Marietta Western Wear first thing tomorrow to get properly outfitted; it's going to get colder they say. I bet you're freezing. Coffee? Hot chocolate? Or how about something stronger? It's after six after all."

Patty Hathaway was in her sixties, as slim and stylish as a catwalk model. Her gray hair was cut into a choppy bob, the ends colored black in a striking contrast to her silver roots. Anything less like the apple-cheeked landlady Zac assumed would run a place like this was hard to imagine.

"No, thank you." Coffee did sound good but it also hinted at informality, at small talk. Zac wanted to make sure any relationship between himself and his landlady remained strictly civil but brief. And he never touched the something stronger.

If Miss Hathaway—no way was he going to call her Aunt Patty—was discomfited she didn't show it. Instead her blue eyes twinkled as she nodded at him. "I'll show you where the kitchen is in case you change your mind."

The door opened into a large wooden-floored hallway, painted a more sober cream Zac was relieved to notice, although the walls were hung with a variety of brightly colored paintings: landscapes, still lifes, and abstracts all jostling for notice. "The kitchen's that way," Patty Hathaway said pointing to an ajar door at the end of the hall. "Our living room is through here, and there's a cozy den in there. You're welcome to use either; make yourself completely at home."

Zac didn't respond and the twinkle in his hostess's eyes intensified as she led him through the hallway and down a back corridor. This one was home to an exhibition's worth of photographs, many black and white with stern-faced family groups featuring mutton-chopped patriarchs. Miss Hathaway stopped outside the white-painted door at the end of the corridor and put her hand on the handle. "Here you are. I hope you'll be comfortable. Yours is the only bedroom on the first floor, the family all sleep upstairs so it's nice and private."

The room she ushered him into was as unlike his usual anonymous motel rooms as a space could be. Thick patterned drapes were already drawn against the winter night and several lamps cast a warm glow over the room. The walls were the same cream as the hallway, the pictures confined to just a couple of large watercolors of the Montana mountains in summer. A blue couch heaped with cushions faced the fireplace, a matching easy chair on either side. A small dining table sat by the window, a cheerful tablecloth draped over it and a bowl filled with fresh fruit placed invitingly in the center.

"Your bedroom is through there." She gestured at another door opposite the window. "And your bath is off that. You should have everything you need but if not just come into the kitchen. There's coffee and snacks in there if you're hungry at any time. Please just help yourself if there's no one around—although either my sister-in-law, Priscilla, or I should be there most of the time. Now, we usually eat at seven after my niece gets home from work, I hope that's okay. You're very welcome to join us but if you're tired then we can put together a tray and bring it to your room."

"Yes, thank you. A tray would be perfect."

She paused, the blue eyes keen. "Of course. I'll leave you to settle in. Remember, there's always a hot drink in the kitchen if you change your mind."

Zac waited until she closed the door behind her before checking out the bedroom and bathroom. The bedroom had the same cozy, comfortable vibe as the living room and the bath boasted a walk-in shower as well as a claw-foot bath. It was a long time since Zac had stayed anywhere that looked so like a home. There was a good reason for that. His hands clenched into fists and he took a deep breath. He might only be here for a few weeks, but he sensed that the sooner he got out of Marietta the better.

"LACEY, PUT THAT down. You'll ruin your appetite." Aunt Patty's words might be stern but her face was anything but as Lacey pulled out a chair and sank into it, the purloined corn muffin, still warm from the oven, in her hand.

"I promise you I won't. Talking nonstop is hungry work."

"Then you must be hungry all the time. How was work today?"

"Great! We're nearly there with all the Bachelor Bake-Off promotional material. We have eight bachelors all signed up and ready to go, tickets are selling well, and there's a real buzz around town."

"It's for a good cause," her aunt said.

Lacey nodded. "It really is and of course everyone really wants to make sure the center is a fitting memorial to Harry." Her smile faded as she remembered the young firefighter so tragically killed. "That's why the station has put so much work and time into helping promote the Bachelor Bake-Off. Not just because Marietta really needs a place like Harry's House, but also because it's the only way we can make sense of something so tragic. Everyone is so enthusiastic it's been a dream to help organize so far. Thanks for agreeing to sponsor a bachelor, Aunt Patty."

"I just hope that brother of yours doesn't let us down; your Aunt Priscilla and I have a reputation to uphold you know. Who's going to buy their wedding cakes from us if Nat produces concrete cookies?"

"You'd better prepare yourself for last place. You know neither Nat nor I inherited the Hathaway baking gene," Lacey warned her aunt. She clasped her hands as excitement quivered through her. "I can't believe Nat's coming to Marietta for a whole month. It almost makes up for him missing Christmas."

"It'll be lovely to see him." Her aunt looked wistful as she turned back to the rich stew bubbling away on the huge range stove. Nat was a real favorite with his aunts and they missed him just as much as his little sister did. Unlike Lacey he didn't live in Marietta anymore, preferring to travel with their musician parents while he developed his own music career. He had spent the whole of his high school senior year in Marietta though, living at Crooked Corner.

"So," Lacey said through a mouthful of corn muffin, "how's the new lodger? No, hang on, let me guess. He's an auditor isn't he? I'm going to go with fiftyish, sporting one of those paunches men get when they spend too long on the road. Graying hair, with a comb-over to hide the bald patch. A good value suit and loafers with tassels on. Am I right?"

"Why don't you see for yourself?" her aunt suggested with a nod toward the door behind Lacey. "He's standing right there. Hello, Zac. Changed your mind about the coffee?"

Lacey choked as the corn muffin stuck in her throat, her cheeks on fire as she turned around, an apology—or a bluff—on her lips, only for the words to dry up as she drank in the vision framed in her aunts' kitchen doorway. No paunchy, graying accountant here, rather over six foot of lean masculinity, dark hair cropped close, darker eyes narrowed.

His well-shaped mouth would have looked made for sin if it wasn't thin with disapproval—disapproval firmly directed right at Lacey.

"Please excuse my niece," Aunt Patty said, smothering a smile unsuccessfully. "She never knows when to stop talking. It's an occupational hazard."

Lacey swallowed the rest of the suddenly dry muffin hastily, and pinned an apologetic look onto her face. "She's right, I do have a bad habit of just saying the first thing that comes into my head and I rarely mean it. I'm a radio host for the local station here in Marietta—well I'm the station manager as well. We're mostly staffed by volunteers…" *Now is the time to stop talking, Lacey*, but the words kept on spilling out. "I'm the only paid member of staff right now but we have ambitions to grow. I do the drive time show but we have a real varied program. Aunt Patty here does a fashion segment and Aunt Priscilla a Saturday morning baking show…" She gulped some scalding hot coffee in an attempt to stop her runaway mouth.

Zac Malone had barely raised an eyebrow in response to her one-woman monologue on the current status of Radio KMCM. "I was wondering if that offer of a cup of coffee was still available?" he addressed Aunt Patty right over Lacey's head.

"Of course, come on in. There's usually coffee on the go here" Aunt Patty indicated the percolator, which was pressed into service fourteen hours a day. "And you'll always find something freshly baked on the second shelf in the pantry. You can help yourself to anything in this kitchen. We just ask guests—and relatives—" she fixed Lacey with a meaningful look "—to stay out of the other kitchen."

"Aunt Patty and Priscilla are bakers," Lacey said, taking pity on the bemused expression on Zac's face. "They have a professional kitchen through there. No matter how enticing the smells, do not follow your nose. The witch in Hansel and Gretel has nothing on these two if you enter their lair."

Silence. She was making quite the impression here. Two strikes down. She had one chance left. "So, Zac. An auditor huh? That must be interesting?"

"Keeps me busy." He poured himself a cup of coffee and nodded over at Aunt Patty. "Thanks for this. I appreciate it." And with that he was gone.

Chapter Two

FIVE DAYS LATER Lacey was still none the wiser about her aunts' latest houseguest. She knew that Zac Malone liked to get up early and go for a run, despite the freezing darkness of a Marietta early morning. He breakfasted in his rooms and had usually left for the Town Hall by 7.30—the same time Lacey was blearily falling out of bed and following her nose to the kitchen and a strong cup of coffee. He arrived back before she'd returned from the station and ate alone in his room, refusing her aunts' invitations to join the family for dinner, to sit with them in the evening, or to accompany them to a talk at the local library.

The only consolation was it wasn't just Lacey he seemed to be avoiding. Several young women had, upon learning he was staying at Crooked Corner, subtly and not so subtly pumped her for information on her hot new houseguest. It seemed Zac Malone was as little interested in making friends at work as he was at home.

"Leave the poor boy alone," Aunt Priscilla told Lacey that evening as Lacey related the latest gossip she'd heard directly from the Town Hall. Her aunt pulled her famous maple cake out of the oven and set it down on the counter top, turning to face her niece with an admonitory expression on her pleasant round face. Priscilla Hathaway was the complete opposite of the sister-in-law with whom she lived and worked. Short and round, her gray hair dyed an improbable chestnut red, she dressed in comfortable slacks and sweatshirts, usually sporting a cheery slogan—a startling contrast to her elegant, fashionable sister-in-law.

"I do leave him alone," Lacey retorted indignantly, her stomach rumbling as the aroma of the cake drifted across the sunny kitchen. "I have no choice in the matter. But it doesn't make any sense. He speaks to no one. All he does is work, sleep, and run. Run in the snow."

"Maybe he likes to be private."

"But it gets lonely traveling around all the time." There was a wistful note in Lacey's voice. She'd spent her childhood traveling from town to city to town, never putting down roots, never fitting in. "He's here for at least six weeks I heard. You'd think he'd want some human contact. He's already been asked out on at least three dates, been invited to several suppers, a pool game, and that poker tournament over at Grey's. He's said no to all of them. Maybe he's nursing a broken heart. Or he's not an auditor at all but on the run."

"That's his business, Lacey. You've no call to be poking around in it."

"I know, I'm sorry, Aunt P." But when that business involved a taciturn if gorgeous stranger right here in her own home the temptation was harder to resist than Aunt Patty's double chocolate fudge caramel cake.

And she never could resist that cake...

Her chance came the very next evening. Both aunts had gone out and, not wanting to entrust their lodger to their niece's cooking, had left supper warming in the oven. The aunts usually put Zac's supper on a tray and took it through to him but Lacey had no intention of acting as his waitress. Instead she set out cutlery at one end of the big scrubbed pine kitchen table, cut up the still-warm bread, and ladled the homemade macaroni and cheese onto two plates, sniffing appreciatively as she did so.

Luckily she was tall, active, and had a healthy metabolism, but she ruefully acknowledged that she'd probably be a good dress and cup size smaller if she lived on her own. Smaller but infinitely more miserable.

She poured water into two tall glasses, took the green salad out of the fridge, and surveyed the table thoughtfully. If she put the jug of flowers on the dresser and put the big overhead light on then the scene looked friendly as opposed to intimate—she didn't want Zac Malone to think she was trying to seduce him after all.

"Okay then," she muttered and took a deep breath, suddenly a little nervous. Tall, dark, and taciturn tended to have that effect on her. "Let's do this." She eyed the tray, ready and waiting on the sideboard. It would take two seconds to load it up and carry it through to him. She turned and marched decisively through the kitchen door before she chickened out and headed down the back corridor to the guest suite, skidding to a halt and knocking loudly on the door before she had a chance to change her mind.

"Come in."

Here went nothing. Lacey turned the handle and pushed the door open a few inches, half twisting around the door so her head and torso were over the threshold but her feet were still firmly planted on the hallway floor. Zac was seated at the table, his laptop open, papers spread all over the floor and table. They were the only personal items in the room; otherwise the sitting room was exactly as it had been when Lacey helped her aunts clean up at the weekend. There was not so much as a stray book or a pair of shoes to be seen. "Hi."

He looked up at that, surprise clear on his face. "Hi."

"The aunts are out. Bingo. Or choir. I can't remember. Anyway they left us dinner, luckily for you. I'm no cook. I'm not even much of a microwaver."

"Right. That's fine."

"So, I thought it might be nice, as the house is so empty, if you wanted, to eat in the kitchen. Both of us. As house-mates. Not a date. Obviously. But you've been here a few days now. So…anyway." She stuttered to a halt and glared at the floor.

Why did he not say anything? Not rescue her from what must be an obvious case of verbal diarrhea?

The silence stretched for several excruciating seconds and then Zac stood up in one decisive movement. "Fine."

"Fine." It was a great start. "It's ready now, if you want to come through." She held the door open for him to exit through, managing to resist a curtsy as he swept past her with barely a nod, then she followed him down the corridor to the kitchen trying not to notice just how nice his rear view was. No wonder every single woman at the Town Hall was asking her for the lowdown on Crooked Corner's latest guest.

Lacey busied herself with passing around the plates and water, hoping that Zac might pick up the conversational baton. No such luck. He simply nodded when she passed him a glass of water, muttered a brief "thanks" when she handed him his plate, and took the seat she indicated wordlessly. Lacey took her own seat at right angles to his and forked up a large mouthful of mac and cheese but, in the awkward silence, the creamy pasta, artfully spiced with Aunt Priscilla's own secret blend of herbs, didn't taste quite as ambrosial as usual.

"Bread?"

"No. Thanks."

"Salt?"

"I'm fine."

"More salad?"

He just shook his head and Lacey regarded him half in despair, half amused. But no way was she giving in; she just needed to try harder. When in doubt drop back on the clichés… "So, Zac, how are you finding Marietta?"

He raised an eyebrow and put down his fork. "Do you really want to know or are you just being polite?"

Lacey stared. "Um, really want to know, I guess."

"Because the polite answer, the answer I think you want to hear, is that Marietta is charming, that I love how quaint it is, the people are so friendly, I've never been anywhere so pretty, and I wish I could stay here forever. Am I right?"

Her chest squeezed painfully at the thinly veiled sarcasm in his voice. That was *exactly* how she felt about Marietta. To her it was perfect in every way from the mountains ringing the town to the selection of local stores lining Main Street. Most importantly it was home. "That's what I think, yes, but I didn't ask you to read my mind and channel my thoughts. I asked you what *you* thought of Marietta. It's no big city but that's why some of us like it." She set her fork down decisively, defensive of her adopted home.

"It's a small town. They're all the same: charm on the surface…" Zac didn't finish but he didn't need to. She understood where he was going.

"It's not just surface! Not at all—in Marietta people really care. Look at this Bachelor Bake-Off I'm involved in…"

"This *what*?"

"Every year we run some kind of Bachelor fundraiser. It's

great publicity; draws people into the area during the post-Christmas slump and provides opportunities for some of the single men to get out and meet people—this is ranch country so there's a lot of single men. It's fun and useful and we always raise lots of money for some good cause."

"I know small-town fundraisers. What is the good cause? Blankets for old donkeys? Bootees for puppies?"

Lacey picked her fork back up and stabbed at a piece of macaroni. *Do not rise to the bait*, she warned herself. She only had herself to blame. She'd wanted to know if there was any substance behind Zac Malone's style and now she had her answer. No. Not unless she counted cynicism as substance.

"Actually this year we're raising money for an after-school club."

She paused but he didn't comment. Lacey went on determinedly. "It's for all the town's kids to use. You're right, no town is nothing but charm and Marietta has its fair share of poverty—and some disadvantaged and problem families. Only in this town we like to help when we can. Harry's House will hopefully give some of those kids a hand while providing a fun place for their peers to hang out too. And if we can have fun while we're raising money for it then that's what we'll do. Harry would have wanted it no other way. I bet he'd have been the first volunteering to be a baking bachelor."

She looked straight at Zac with a defiant tilt of her chin and to her surprise saw the cynical gleam had gone from his brown eyes. He had leaned forward while she spoke, focused on every word.

"That sounds like a really good idea. What will the after-school club do?"

Lacey blinked. A genuine-sounding question. Wonders would never cease. "It'll be open before and after school and at weekends. Somewhere kids can do their homework, hang out. There'll be workshops and classes, fun things as well as educational, sometimes both. My aunts will do baking classes, I'll do some film and documentary workshops, plus there will be woodworking, help with homework for those who need it, that kind of thing. It's something the town has wanted to do for a long time but Harry's death kind of made it a priority. It just seems like the right way to remember him."

"What happened?"

"Hit and run," she said flatly. "He stopped to change a tire for an elderly couple when it happened. That was the kind of guy he was, always helping others."

"I'm sorry. Were you close?"

"Not really but you know small towns." She shrugged. "We all know each other to some degree. Harry was at school with my brother, Nat, for a year. He was a good guy."

"He sounds it, and it sounds like a good project. Let me know when it's on and I'll bid for a cookie or whatever. Every child needs somewhere to go especially when things get tough at home." His voice was bleak and he pushed his plate away. "Thanks for dinner, Lacey. That was delicious but I have some work to do. See you around."

And while Lacey was still searching for something to say he strode out of the room leaving her staring at his empty place, no closer to knowing Zac Malone than she had been when he'd first sat down.

But nor was she ready to give up. For a moment there he'd been interested in what she had to say and that Zac, eyes alight with interest, his focus on her, was a Zac Lacey wanted to see more of. But she sensed opportunities would be slim and she'd have to tread carefully. No matter what the aunts said she could be subtle when she turned her mind to it and right now her mind was firmly made up.

Zac Malone was a mystery she was going to crack.

Chapter Three

Z AC WAS SURROUNDED by paperwork. Spreadsheets populated his laptop screen, reports piled high on the table and the floor. Marietta had grown so rapidly that the Town Hall's systems had failed to keep up. He was there to audit the finances and suggest the right method and software to see the town safely through the period of growth, install them, and train all the users. Work he should—he usually could—do in his sleep. Time-consuming and meticulous? Yes. Difficult? Not at all.

But it was difficult to concentrate when messy, unwanted emotions were jostling around his brain demanding his attention. Memories he'd spent the last twelve years trying to suppress. And worst of all, it was his fault they'd resurfaced. He'd allowed himself to get companionable with the youngest of Crooked Corner's inhabitants and then lowered his guard when Lacey mentioned the scheme to set up a club for the town's kids. He'd even experienced a tinge of curiosity about the Bachelor Bake-Off—even though it was the kind of cute community gathering he would usually take a mile-long detour to avoid.

And, let's face it: he was also experiencing a certain amount of curiosity about his dining companion of the evening. He might have a no dating on assignment rule but he was still flesh and blood, and Lacey Hathaway was an attractive girl. Tall, leggy, and blonde with the kind of curves women in California spent their time exercising and starving off their frames—but the kind of curves that were nice and easy on a man's eyes. Not that Lacey seemed aware of how attractive she was.

The long blonde hair was usually scooped up in a messy ponytail, no makeup lined the candid blue eyes, and she seemed to live in a uniform of blue jeans and soft sweaters. Zac stared at his computer screen barely taking in the long lists of figures. That was far more information than he'd known about the receptionist at the last motel he'd stayed in. He wasn't even sure if her name had been Marla or Marlene. Maybe Maria.

But he couldn't help but *be* aware in this case despite his very best efforts to the contrary, probably because Lacey insisted on being noticed. She was everywhere—her spicy cinnamon and vanilla scent perfumed the whole house, her scarves and books and keys and bags littered every room, and she spent half her time tearing through the house like a tornado searching for whatever she'd last mislaid. She talked all the time. Even here, shut away in his private rooms, he could hear her yelling a question to her aunts, singing along to the radio or laughing—a surprisingly low, melodious laugh that made even the most resistant listener crack a smile in return.

It would be all too easy to dismiss her, put her in the same box as all the other happy-go-lucky, charmed people who floated through life never noticing anything that could burst their comfortable bubble. But there had been a look in her eyes when she leapt to her town's defense, a wistful loneliness that he recognized all too well. A look he'd seen in the mirror until he'd trained every inch of weakness out of himself.

And the project she was helping fundraise for did sound pretty amazing. It was the kind of project that could make all the difference to a troubled kid's life. The kind of project that would have made all the difference to his life. His life back then. His life right now was pretty damn fine. Under control. His control.

Zac pushed his chair back restlessly. This was exactly why he steered clear of places like Marietta, exactly why he preferred the anonymous monotony of a chain motel. He could rock up, do his job, and leave with no thoughts more troubling than where he was heading to next. But here, in this warm, cozy sitting room, knowing coffee was brewing in the kitchen down the hall, that freshly made doughnuts and apple cake were waiting in the pantry, that there were three friendly faces he could just sit down next to and make conversation with or not depending on his mood... Here it was far too hard to concentrate on the matter at hand, far too hard to shut out the memories knocking insistently at his brain. Memories he had no intention of letting in.

He shot a glance at his watch and sighed. It was still early, barely eight p.m. He couldn't work, wasn't much of one for TV, avoided bars, had already eaten, and had no idea of what—if anything—happened in Marietta at night. But he couldn't sit here any longer, staring at the screen and trying not to think of the past.

Zac grabbed the warm, padded jacket he'd picked up just a few days ago and pulled on the equally new waterproof boots, their tread guaranteed to protect against all but the slipperiest of ice. He needed fresh air, no matter how cold that air; nor did he care that the snow was once more falling steadily from the winter-dark sky.

He'd heard the two elder Ms. Hathaways come in a few minutes earlier and knew the family had all congregated in the kitchen. It really was the heart of the home, a warm chintzy space with no pretensions to fashion. Crooked Corner's kitchen was painted a sunny yellow, the wooden cabinets a warm cream. Flowery blinds matched the oilskin tablecloth that covered the vast table dominating the room, a table used just as much for mixing cakes, tapping away at a laptop, drinking coffee around, and gossiping as it was for eating at.

A noticeboard was covered in fliers for local events and recipes ripped out from magazines and photos. More magazines were piled up on the old dresser and vases and jugs were dotted around, filled with an eclectic selection of dried and fresh flowers, dried leaves, and twigs. It was always busy, an endless stream of neighbors, customers, and local kids streaming through for coffee, cake, and a chat with one or the other of the elder Ms. Hathaways. There were moments when Zac almost wished he could just avail himself of the open invitation to pour himself a cup, pull up a chair, and allow himself to become part of this warm family. For a while at least.

The voices were a little louder than usual as he exited his room—an undercurrent of worry in the mingled tones—and Zac's footsteps faltered as he reached the kitchen door. Was everything okay? Should he check in and see if there was anything he could do? He might not want to get pulled any further into this family but he still had his basic good manners. He paused, torn.

"I can't believe he's done this!" That was Lacey, her rich voice unmistakable even if it was shriller than usual. "He *knew* how important this is. Not just to me but to everyone. It's like he's forgotten us. Forgotten Marietta."

A calming murmur seemed to have no effect as Lacey exclaimed, "No, he's exactly the same as Mom and Dad: music first, family second. And it's not just us he's let down—the Bake-Off people are counting on him too. I don't know what to do. I can't believe Nat's not coming home." And then he heard a gulp that sounded horribly like a swallowed sob.

Zac wavered. It was just family business. No need to intrude. He should just keep going. A nice, cold walk in the dark and snow. He was supposed to be clearing his head not muddling it further. But somehow his footsteps led him not past the ajar kitchen door and down the hall to the front door and solitude, but into the warm kitchen where three worried faces turned to face him. Lacey's eyes were suspiciously wet although her cheeks were flushed with indignation.

He leaned against the doorframe. "Sorry, I don't mean to intrude but is there anything I can do to help?"

It was a polite offer. Zac didn't really expect it to be taken up in any way. He certainly didn't expect the three women to look at him at first in surprise and then in hope, nor did he expect a speculative gleam to light up Lacey Hathaway's fine blue eyes or a smile to curve her full mouth as she stared at him as if he were Christmas, her birthday, and a chocolate hamper all rolled into one. "Zac! Of course. You're single aren't you?"

"Yes," he said cautiously. "But I don't see…"

"Thank goodness," she breathed and turned to her aunts, her face alight. "Aunt Patty, Aunt Priscilla, we have our bachelor!"

Our *what*?

Zac took an instinctive step back.

"We were talking about it earlier," Lacey said. "Remember? The Bachelor Bake-Off I'm helping organize? The Crooked Corner are is sponsoring a bachelor and I'm planning to video the whole learning to bake process and the Bake-Offs themselves to try and raise the profile of the after-school club. The plan is to get some out of town interest, which will hopefully lead to grants toward equipment and running costs. My brother, Nat, had promised to come home and be our bachelor but he's just called and canceled…" Her voice faltered.

Aunt Priscilla took up the tale. "Nat's a very talented musician and he's been asked to be the support act on a really prestigious tour. We're delighted for him." The glance she gave her niece was full of meaning. Meaning Lacey was obviously not intending to take.

"*I'm* not," Lacey said. "He was supposed to come and stay with us at Christmas but bailed to go and play with Mom and Dad, and now he's let us down again. He's going to be exactly the same as they are. Always on the road, every concert more important than promises or family or staying in one place for more than a minute. But if you stepped in for him then we could at least salvage something." Her face was bright with hope.

"Step in and do what?"

"Enter the contest of course. As our baking bachelor."

"I don't bake." There were plenty of other reasons why this was a terrible idea, Zac knew, but the obvious was all he could articulate right now. This was why he hated small towns. He'd been here for less than a week and was already being inveigled into community life. Another week and he'd be helping preschoolers learn to read and taking fruit baskets into the hospital. No one even spoke to him in most cities let alone looked at him as if he was their salvation.

"Oh, that doesn't matter at all; in fact it's part of the fun. Nat can't even make toast but Aunt Patty and Aunt Priscilla bake. Very, very well. They will teach you three recipes. One for each round. I mean, they will if you agree." Now pleading had joined the hope in her face, Lacey's eyes big and round and focused right on him. Zac took another step back.

"I know I said I'd buy a cookie or something and I'm happy to make a donation but that's as far as I'm prepared to go. I don't live here, I don't do community or bake sales or fundraisers, and I might be single but I like it that way and I'm certainly not intending to join some bachelor auction." His stomach turned at the thought of it. Of all that attention. People talking about him.

Lacey didn't blink. "Oh no, it's the things you bake that get bought, not you. We did a bachelor auction last year. It was really successful but we don't like to repeat ourselves. Honestly, Zac, it's fine. Like I said, there's a lot of single men out on the ranches and the winter can be a quiet time for them. This is just a bit of fun over the winter, which mingles raising money with the opportunity for single people who want to meet people to do so. That's all. Taking part doesn't mean you'll be targeted as ready and available."

Zac eyed her suspiciously. He didn't believe that for one second. He'd met several women since he'd been here who, straight after introduction had slid their gaze right down to his wedding ring finger and then, noting its bare state, slid back up to meet his eyes with an obvious invitation. It seemed that women in Marietta were not shy about coming forward. He had no intention of encouraging them further.

"So why not ask one of those single ranchers to step in?"

"We could do, I suppose." She looked so ludicrously crestfallen Zac almost—almost—felt guilty for turning her down. "It's just you are right here; it makes filming and baking lessons so much easier. We wanted someone from Crooked Corner to be involved. I was so happy when Nat said yes and we kind of organized ourselves around him. You being here at this very moment seemed heaven-sent."

"I don't really have the time." It was a lame reason and he knew it. Why wasn't he just saying a flat no and leaving? But good manners—and, much as he hated to admit it, the hope in Lacey's eyes—kept him standing awkwardly in the doorway.

"All the Bake-Offs are on Saturdays… The Town Hall shuts at weekends so you're free."

"Lacey." Priscilla patted her niece's arm. "Don't bully the poor boy. We'll figure something out."

"But the first round is in just over a week. This Bake-Off has really pulled the town together after Harry's death. Goodness knows we needed something fun to focus on. Zac, before you decide will you just come see the house, see what we're trying to do? If you still feel uncomfortable after that I promise not to say another word…" Lacey looked imploringly at him.

No. Absolutely not. But, just like an hour earlier when she'd shown up in his room and suggested he eat dinner with her, Zac found he didn't quite know how to say no to Lacey Hathaway, not when she had that pleading look on her face. "Fine."

"Really? That's amazing. You won't regret it I promise."

What had he done? "Fine I'll take a look at the house, that's all. Nothing more. If I were you I'd get a list of alternate bachelor bakers together and get phoning because you're going to need it tomorrow," he warned but Lacey just grinned.

"I know, I know, but just wait till tomorrow. Wait till you see it and then decide. Oh, thank you, Zac. I can't tell you how much I appreciate this!" And before he knew what she was doing, before he had a chance to step away, Lacey danced forward and hugged him. A brief hug, her hands light on his shoulders but still. A hug. Zac froze, her cinnamon scent enveloping him, the softness of her hair still imprinted on his chin as Lacey released him and stepped back, glowing.

He had to get out of this house, this kitchen, before he found himself promising to cook a four-course meal for every single woman in Marietta. "Right. I'm just going for a walk so I'll see you tomorrow. To look at the house."

"Yes, yes tomorrow. Better get an apron ready because I promise you, you'll take one look at that house and you will be ready to start baking!"

Chapter Four

LACEY PULLED AT her sweater nervously. She'd seen neither hide nor hair of Zac since he'd walked in on her dramatic scene the evening before—she'd probably scared him away with that hug. Lacey closed her eyes, as if she could block out the memory along with her sight. What had she been thinking? She was a talker not a hugger; she saved her tactile moments for her family not for complete strangers. Complete strangers who stood there as if they were hewn out of granite as she pressed herself against them.

"Okay, Hathaway," she muttered. "Remember to keep your hands to yourself." The flush that swept over her as she remembered just how much of him her hands had actually touched was completely because her aunts had turned the thermostat way up too high and nothing to do with how firm Zac's shoulders had been under her fingers. No, nothing to do with that at all.

Lacey turned to the window and took a deep breath. Calm, professional, and persuasive, not babbling and inappropriate. Easy.

It was a glorious winter's morning, the sun gleaming in a sky so blue it almost fooled her that summer was here—until she noticed the snow on the branches outside the window or stepped outside into the freezing temperatures. She loved this season: the crunchiness of the snow underfoot, hot chocolates and sleigh rides and ice-skating on the lake.

But she loved spring too with its promise of warmth and growth, the gradual shedding of layers until winter clothes were consigned to the closet in all their bulk. As for summer, hayrides and swimming, meadows filled with flowers and the warmth of the sun on her bare skin, often Lacey loved summer best of all. Until she got to fall—that was—with its dramatic coloring and crispness. Face it, she loved all the seasons. She'd hated it when her parents had spent too long in southern states where winter required merely a hoodie not a thick jacket.

There. She could chat about the weather. A nice, safe, non-body-contact topic of conversation.

Zac was already in the kitchen when Lacey finally left the sanctuary of her bedroom and headed down the stairs. He was weekend ready in a pair of perfectly tailored black jeans that Lacey bet cost more than all her many pairs put together and a beautiful gray cashmere sweater that managed to be smart, define every muscle in his arms, and give him a far more relaxed look than the crisp shirts and suits he favored for work. Not that she was becoming an expert on his wardrobe; no, she was a trained journalist. She spotted details; that was all.

Horribly aware her cheeks were blazing warm and probably an attractive bright red, Lacey allowed her hair to sweep over her face as she walked past Zac with as breezy a "Morning!" as she could manage. There was no sign of either aunt but that was no surprise. Saturday was a workday at Crooked Corner Cakes. She poured coffee into her travel cup, added some half and half, and snagged a still-warm apple and cinnamon muffin from the basket on the table. "Okay." She plastered on a smile—not too bright, she'd scared him enough already. "Shall we get going?"

"Sure."

Obviously they were back to monosyllabic answers. Never mind. Once Zac Malone had seen what the town had in mind for Harry's House he would be positively garrulous. And, once they'd seen the house, maybe they could take a circuitous route back to Crooked Corner and give him a chance to see the town at its best; it was still dark when he went to work and dark again when he came home. But Marietta buzzing with Saturday vibes was a fun place to be. Even Zac would surely find something positive in the friendly, warm atmosphere.

Lacey opened the pantry door and stopped. Something was wrong. The shelves were groaning under the weight of ingredients and baked goods as usual, nothing seemed out of place, the small room scrupulously clean, no spillages or suspicious smells. And yet...

She moved the door. Nothing. Not a squeak.

"The pantry door! It's stopped squeaking."

"It just needed oiling that was all." Zac padded up alongside her so silently she hadn't noticed and she jumped at his sudden proximity.

"You oiled it? How?"

"With the oil can. I mended the hinge on the back door as well and straightened that shelf."

Lacey stared fascinated at the shelf above the radiator. It had always been a little wonky. Nat had hung it last time he came to visit and although better than his baking skills his DIY was a little haphazard.

"The perfect lodger," she said. "Careful or the aunts will draw up a never-ending list of jobs. None of us is that practical; we tend to hope for the best until it breaks. Where did you learn to do that anyway? Accountancy school?"

"I took care of the house growing up. Learned a few things."

She now knew one thing about Zac Malone; he was handy with a toolbox. It felt like progress. Lacey didn't want to analyze why this pleased her so much, turning briskly to wipe the thought from her mind. "Thanks, Zac, the aunts will be so pleased. Right, are you ready? Marietta awaits!"

LACEY WASN'T OFTEN at a loss for words. But she was

unaccountably tongue-tied as she and Zac stepped off the porch onto the driveway and made their way onto Bramble Lane. *Pull yourself together, Hathaway*, she told herself sternly.

"This is Bramble Lane, but I guess you know that already. It's the historic heart of the village. Some of the houses are as old as the state of Montana itself. Have you noticed Bramble House by the park? That huge old Victorian on the corner? It's a B&B now; it's still lovely but once upon a time it was the fanciest private house in town." When in doubt just say anything and Marietta was a subject she was comfortable with.

Lacey's confidence returned as she led them along the sidewalk, pointing out sights of local or historical interest while she planned their route. It was only a short walk if they took a right turn up 4th and then a left onto Church Avenue where the house was—nice and near the school district, an easy, safe walk for the prospective users. "The schools are just there, right near the community park and the recreation center. It's a really nice park. Baseball field, plenty of space to hang out, to picnic."

His gaze as they passed the elementary school was amused. "Is this where you went to school? I can just see you now, ribbons on the end of your pigtails, skipping down the street."

So could Lacey. She'd imagined it often enough. "No. I only managed two years of high school here."

"Really? You're such a poster girl for the town I assumed you were born and bred Marietta, copper running in your veins instead of blood."

Lacey smiled as she instinctively looked back over to the stately Copper Mountain, snow-covered now as it stood guard over the town as it had done since the first pioneers built the first homestead, since the original inhabitants had hunted through the rich mountains. "A little bit of copper, yes; both my parents are from here but they left before I was born."

"But you live with your aunts?" His voice was cautious now, as if wary of treading onto sensitive territory. It must seem odd, a grown woman of twenty-five living with two women in their late sixties, just as odd as a teenager of sixteen voluntarily choosing to.

"My parents travel a lot. They're musicians, the Copper Mountain trio? And yes, there *are* only two of them. They're kind of well known, if you like folk music. They believe in taking music to the masses so we didn't really live anywhere, not long enough to put down any roots that is."

"So you traveled the country as a child and decided Marietta was the best the world had to offer?" He sounded amused now, a little superior, and Lacey's hackles rose.

"Traveled the *world*," she corrected him. "They played all over Europe several times, we went to Australia and New Zealand twice, toured most of South America, Japan. I had more stamps in my passport by the time I was thirteen than most Americans manage in a lifetime. But you know what I realized? A hotel room is a hotel room, a concert venue has the same smell, the same stage, the same backstage area in Paris as it does in Santa Fe. Sightseeing isn't so much fun when you've been living out of a suitcase for months on end and there are times when you wake up in Phoenix and genuinely can't remember that you spent three months there several years before. Or worse, you know you're spending the winter in Nashville and you can't wait to get back to school and meet up with the friends you made there last time you stayed. Only those friends have grown up and changed and you don't fit in anymore."

Lacey paused and swallowed. "Marietta is my home," she said quietly. "And in my book that makes it the best the US or the world has to offer."

Zac's brows drew together at her words but he didn't answer and they continued to walk in a silence that was oddly companionable until they reached Church Avenue and the house earmarked for the afterschool club.

It was a perfectly ordinary house. Faded and peeling but painted white with a green trim, a porch out front overlooking the graveled driveway and front lawn. It was pretty run-down but there was nothing that some hard work and commitment couldn't sort out—along with the twenty-five thousand dollars it was estimated the repairs would cost.

"This is it," she said, scanning Zac's face for a clue as to what he was thinking. "The house was donated to the town and the Chamber of Commerce have offered it to us to use for a club—as you can imagine, something this run-down right in the middle of town isn't great for tourism. But the deal is we only have ninety days to get it cleaned up and made fit for purpose, otherwise it gets sold off to any commercial concern who wants it—and the clock's ticking. Hence the Bachelor Bake-Off. If we can get the money we need then there is just enough time, if the community pitches in, to make the deadline. But it's tight and every cent really does count. One less bachelor means less stuff to bid on, less to see, that the whole thing is that little bit less of an event. That's why we need you."

Lacey led him up the porch stairs and knocked on the faded green door, Zac following on more slowly behind her. The door swung open and a tall, graying man in his forties greeted her with a smile.

"If it isn't my favorite talk show host," he said standing aside to let her pass by him into the house. "How are you doing, Lacey?"

"I'm good, thanks, Chief." She stopped and looked around at the bare floorboards and the peeling walls. "How's it going?"

"There's a lot to do, can't be denied, but it's not impossible. How can I help you, Lacey? Do you need something from me for the Bake-Off?"

"Actually I would like to interview all the judges at some point, Chief Hale, but if it's okay right now I'd like to show

Zac around and let him see what we're trying to do here. I'm trying to inspire him to be the Crooked Corner bachelor. Nat had to drop out. Zac, Chief Hale is going to be one of the judges for the Bake-Off."

"I'm the one it will be easiest to impress. I appreciate a nice cake but I don't know too much about the process. It's the other three who know what they're looking for; they're all professionals after all. Who else is lined up to take part, do you know, Lacey?"

Lacey chewed her lip while she thought. "Harry's family wanted to be involved and so they have sponsored Avery Wainright. Do you know him? He's a rodeo rider. Tyler Carter from the gym has been put forward by his employees who seem very keen to watch him bake! Um, I believe Wes St. Claire is another. I don't know him at all but apparently he's working here over the winter and his dad has sponsored him on behalf of the family firm for a bit of local PR, which is great. Plus Matthew West; it's always good to have a medic involved—even if he is more used to dealing with animals. With the Crooked Corner bachelor that's five and there are another three I just can't remember off hand. So eight bachelors at five hundred dollars each gives us four thousand dollars before we even start. I bet we can meet target, Chief."

ZAC STOOD JUST inside the hall while Lacey chatted. He

looked around at the dirty woodwork, the bare staircase, and the exposed wires. It would take a lot of work to bring this old house up to scratch: work, time, and money. All for a bunch of kids. His hands clenched into fists and for the first time in a long time his chest ached, a mixture of nostalgia and sadness. Nostalgia for the years he'd been part of a happy, loving family. A family just like the ones he passed every day, kids swung onto dads' shoulders, holding hands with their moms, hats pulled low and hands mittened against the cold. Sadness for the way it ended so abruptly, for a boy forced to grow up far too soon. And hope. Hope because a place like this might have made all the difference to a boy like him.

It would make a difference thanks to the dedication of the two people standing before him and the nameless, countless others who gave their time and energy.

"Zac!" The impatience in Lacey's voice suggested this wasn't the first time she'd called his name. "Do you want to look around?"

"Fine. Lead the way."

He pushed off the wall and nodded at the Chief before following Lacey into the sun-filled back room. It was a huge space, windows looking out at the garden below. "We're planning a kitchen in here," she said, a sweeping gesture indicating the back wall. "It'll host a breakfast club before school and in vacation time. It'll be filled with healthy snacks for after school and the aunts will run weekend baking and simple cooking lessons. They plan for every child who comes here to be able to grow up knowing five simple recipes and be able to make bread and a layer cake." She wrinkled her nose. "It's a fine sentiment but they never did manage to teach me or Nat; maybe we were too old and too used to room service by the time they got their hands on us."

"It's a good plan," he agreed. He had lived on cans and mac and cheese from a box for a couple of years until he'd managed to teach himself to cook a few cheap and nutritious meals. He was probably the only adult in the US who had bad memories of packaged mac and cheese.

"Okay, then over here is the old living room. We're hoping to turn it into a studio." Lacey led Zac back into the hallway and into a big square room that ran the whole length of the house. "The plan is to hold martial arts, dance classes, drama, anything really—if there's someone qualified to teach it then they'll run it."

A planned small office and reception area completed the first floor and Lacey informed him that upstairs would hold a quiet room with desks for homework, a chill-out room with games and beanbags, and a library and reading room. "There's an attic as well so there's room to develop further," she said. "And of course there's the garden, which will have vegetable plots where the kids will be encouraged to learn about plants and gardening, as well as hoops and other outdoor games."

She turned to him, eyes wide with hope. "I know Marietta looks prosperous but like anywhere else it has its fair share of kids who need a hand or just some space for many reasons. Some have loving families but they're just feeling off-kilter; others, well others have been dealt a rougher hand. But they all need somewhere. Look, a Bachelor Bake-Off might sound a little crazy to you but it's a great way to bring the community together and to raise awareness of Harry's House. Will you consider helping?"

Zac couldn't answer. Not yet. He stayed away from any ties from choice. No family, no close groups of friends, no binds to anyone or anything. It was easier, safer that way. If he said yes he'd be making a commitment to this place, a temporary commitment but a commitment all the same. But how could he say no when he knew just how life-changing a place like this could be?

"What would be involved? I don't sign anything without reading the small print first."

A huge smile split Lacey's face. It was as if the sun had come out. "Nothing too onerous I promise. There's three rounds. You bake cookies for the first, easing you into it, a pie for the second, and a cake for the third. No novelty aprons although I think that was touted as a possibility but you get off easy. If you agree that is," she added quickly but the gleam in her eyes suggested she was confident of his capitulation. "It starts a week today and then the two Saturdays after, finishing off with afternoon tea at The Graff."

"How much are you hoping to make?" Maybe he could just make a donation instead, assuage his conscience at second hand.

"Twenty-five thousand minimum," Lacey said. "Each bachelor costs five hundred dollars to enter and then each event has some kind of fundraising event attached to it. Plus we'll be soliciting donations from some of the town's wealthier individuals so we're confident we can make it."

He could easily afford to reimburse the Crooked Corner for the bachelor sponsorship. "Couldn't you just ask those wealthy individuals for donations and dispense with the whole baking part?"

"I guess, but we want the club to feel like it belongs to the town. This way everyone can contribute whether it's bidding on a cookie or buying a raffle ticket. Look, Zac, it doesn't matter that you can't bake; that's kind of the point. Nobody will be judging you, well, they will but not in a mean-spirited way. Besides, this is your opportunity to prove that the auditor stereotype is wrong."

"That we're middle-aged with the spreading middle and receding hairline to match?" Zac said dryly watching with satisfaction as the color rose in Lacey's cheeks.

"You may have noticed that I have a tendency to talk nonsense," she said with dignity. "But you have to admit people don't expect auditors to be as young and as..." She stopped abruptly, her cheeks reddening even further.

Zac took pity on her, not sure if he wanted to know what

she was going to say or not. As stuffy? Or something more complimentary? His mind flew back to the hug the night before, how soft she had been, how warm. The scent of her still lingered in his mind, a sensual memory. Hands off, he reminded himself. Even if he was to break his no dating while working rule he instinctively knew Lacey Hathaway wasn't the type of girl to enjoy a brief no-strings dalliance. No, she needed wooing, romance, sleigh rides in the snow and picnics by the lake. Someone to adore her, to find her babbling endearing. Someone who wanted to settle down and become part of the town she loved so much—not a scarred, embittered loner.

It would be dangerous to agree to be one of the bachelors. To be part of this place even for a short while. He didn't need reminding of everything he had turned his back on, although not until they had so comprehensively turned their backs on him. His gaze flew to the battered old house. Would this community have left him alone to fall or would someone, some people, have extended the helping hand he had once so desperately needed? The only thing he knew for sure is they were prepared to try. And if so, knowing how much it mattered, how could he stand aloof?

"I'd need help. I have never baked in my life."

"The aunts will jump at the chance," she assured him. "They love teaching people to bake. Aunt Patty actually learned at a proper Parisian patisserie school. She has mad pastry skills. Aunt Priscilla was in charge of cooking at the family ranch when Uncle Bill was still alive. She could make enough bread to feed twenty cowboys before breakfast and have five different pies on the table by lunch! They'll be so happy to teach you, and it will stop them trying to get me to make a decent cake. After several flat cakes and soggy pies I told them I was happy to stay on the eating side of the process. The baking gene just plain passed me by."

"Let me get this straight," Zac said slowly. "You want me to learn to bake in a week, enter a competition, and let people judge my efforts but you just gave up trying to learn?"

"A family doesn't need three professional bakers!"

"In that case I'll make a deal with you, Lacey Hathaway. I'll be your bachelor but you can learn to bake right along-side me."

LACEY STARED AT Zac in disbelief. He was joking, right? But he hadn't shown any signs of being the jokey type so far. "But...I'm already involved. I'm documenting the process, remember?"

"It would be a great hook for your radio show and the documentary, more of an immersive process. You can suffer along with me. Come on, Lacey. No one will even be judging you."

"I..." For once she couldn't find any words let alone the right ones—and not just because of Zac's unexpected suggestion. The way laughter brought out the gold flecks in his brown eyes, the realization that when he smiled he had a small but perfect dimple at the corner of his mouth, the tightness in her chest when all his intensity was directed solely at her discombobulated her in a completely unexpected way.

"Let's make it interesting." His voice was a gravelly purr, which weakened both Lacey's legs and her resolve. How had she thought this man stuffy? He was lethal. It was as if Clark Kent had whipped off his glasses and the real man stood there, although instead of tight lycra he was devastating in his black coat and jeans.

"Interesting how?" She forced herself to concentrate as he offered the wager. Lacey had an older brother; she was by no means defenseless when it came to competition and high stakes.

"We'll hold our own mini bake-off the morning of each fundraiser. The aunts can judge. The loser pays an agreed donation to the center each time. Fifty dollars, say?"

Another guaranteed one hundred and fifty dollars for the center. With time so tight and so much work to be done there was no way she could turn it down. And Zac was right, it would add a nice extra dimension to the publicity she had planned. Sure she was featuring the Bake-Off on her radio show and planning to interview all the bachelors but anyone who was interested in Marietta probably already knew about it. The short documentaries she was planning were destined for the internet and she was really hoping to get support from further afield with them. A personal stake would surely make them that much more powerful.

"Okay." Her heart was hammering fast. Lacey swallowed and before she could think her next words through carried on. "But let's make the stakes a little more personal." She couldn't believe she'd said the words out loud and as the gleam in Zac's eyes intensified she fought the urge to backtrack.

"More personal?" he drawled, soft and slow and dangerous. Lacey's stomach clenched.

"If I win, then I get to show you my Marietta," she said quickly. "In all its small-town charm and quaintness. If you win…"

"If I win then I get to choose."

"Choose what?"

"I don't know yet. But be sure of one thing, Lacey. You'll find out in the fullness of time because I really, really don't like to lose."

Chapter Five

"RIGHT." AUNT PRISCILLA folded her arms and stared sternly at Lacey and Zac. Lacey tried very hard not to meet Zac's eye or she knew she would start giggling. It was hard not to feel like a naughty teenager after three lectures about hygiene and a health and safety talk that had included a whiteboard and diagrams showing all the many ways a person could injure themselves in the kitchen.

Zac had started the morning as his usual unreachable self, aloof as if he felt himself above the proceedings, but by the time Aunt Priscilla had shown them a drawing of a person impaling themselves on the handle of a wooden spoon, which had improbably been left stick-up in a jar on the floor he had melted—much like the butter that apparently was quite capable of scalding a person so badly they would be maimed for life.

"You didn't warn me this would be so dangerous," he murmured, his breath warm on Lacey's neck. She shivered despite the warmth of the kitchen, his proximity bringing her out in goose bumps. What was going on? She wasn't usually a sucker for a handsome face and an attitude. When she imagined finally falling in love and settling down she always thought it would be with someone kind and safe, maybe a little homely but with a good heart. Someone who wanted a family, children, and security and was happy with the small things in life—just like she was.

At least if she was developing an inappropriate crush it was with someone who would be gone in a couple of months. Maybe that was why her stomach kept turning over and she was all too aware of the soft tan of his wrists, the strength in his hands. It was a safe crush. And nothing to do with the teasing smile in his eyes or the feeling that she was in a very exclusive club indeed now Zac Malone had decided to be friendly toward her.

"I had no idea," she whispered back as soon as her aunt's back was safely turned. "I always thought the cake mix was the tastiest part but after that lecture on salmonella I'll never sneak a lick of the spoon again."

"Right." Her aunt whirled round and fixed them both with a gimlet stare. They were practicing in the professional kitchen. The large, sleek space was all machines and stainless steel and thermometers and blowtorches and state-of-the-art ovens. As soon as they set foot inside it seemed that both aunts transformed from the sweet women Lacey knew and loved to scary reality show judges. "Both of you take up your positions by your workstations. It's time to start on this week's tasks. Cookies."

"Cookies," Lacey echoed as she took in the three bowls, sieve, two spatulas, three spoons, four knives, and cookie tsheets. It all seemed a little like overkill. Really, how hard could it be? She hadn't had much baking success in the past it was true, but small children made cookies all the time. It couldn't be beyond her. Could it?

"The secret to a successful cookie is air and the temperature of the butter," Aunt Patty said. She'd stood to one side during the lengthy kitchen orientation but now she strode to stand between the workstations looking every inch the elegant catwalk model she once had been: tall, slim and, as always, dressed one hundred times more fashionably than her great-niece.

Lacey looked down at her trusty blue jeans, today teamed with a soft pink sweater. Would she be able to pull off swishy silk trousers in navy and gold with a matching slouchy jacket? She suspected not. And she certainly couldn't pull off the spike heels her aunt was never without. "Baking is alchemy. Our job is to turn these ingredients—" she held up a stick of butter in one hand and a bag of sugar in the other with a flourish as if they were valuable auction items "—into culinary gold. Too much air and protein and you get a soft, spreadable cookie. But that's not what we want. We want a good snap. What do we want?"

"A good snap," Lacey parroted obediently, all too aware of Zac's sardonic glance.

"Teacher's pet," he mouthed and she flashed him a smile

before turning back to her aunt.

"That's right because we are starting with a classic cookie, a recipe handed down to me by my Scottish mother, that's your great-grandmother, Lacey. She was a wonderful cook and she was particularly known for her shortbread. A perfect pairing of butter, sugar, and flour. Made correctly it can be cut into a variety of shapes, which makes it a good choice for seasonal cookies. Zac, you will be baking twelve stars, twelve hearts, and twelve of the classical rectangles."

It was Lacey's turn to smirk in Zac's direction as he said, "That's thirty-six cookies," in an apprehensive voice.

"Shortbread is, of course, a classic for a reason," Aunt Patty carried on, ignoring him. "Not only is it a very satisfactory cookie to eat but it is also very easy to make. So we are going to customize the shortbread recipe to add a little variety and interest to your bake. Zac, what would you like? Lavender is very popular in shortbread, or we could be a little adventurous. Chili chocolate? Coffee and walnut? Cardamom and pistachio?"

Zac looked helplessly at Lacey who smiled as guilelessly as she could back at him, refusing to feel even slightly guilty for embroiling him in this workshop on his day off. Besides, he would probably have gone for a run and worked, Saturday or no Saturday. She'd actually done him a favor.

"They all sound good," he said. "But maybe a little fancy for a beginner. Chocolate chip is always good. We need a crowd pleaser don't we?"

"Maybe you're right," Aunt Patty admitted with a wistful look at the extensive herb rack. "But it still needs something to make it zing. Lemon zest?"

"How about orange," Lacey suggested. "Chocolate and orange go well together."

"Chocolate chip orange shortbread. Perfect. Now, Zac." Aunt Patty put the butter and sugar down with a thud. "The Crooked Corner has a reputation around here. We are known for the excellence of our bakes. You don't want to let us down do you?"

"No, ma'am," he responded promptly.

"And, Lacey? I'm glad to see you here at last. Your great-grandmother turns in her grave every time you buy ready to bake cookies. Let's try and give her some rest, hmmm?"

"Yes, ma'am." Lacey almost saluted but managed to catch herself in time.

The next hour was a bewildering mixture of instructions, flour, and bits of butter. The butter had to be cold, which made mixing it into the smooth paste the aunts insisted on difficult without a mixer. "Your grandmother didn't use a mixer," Aunt Patty said looking scandalized when Lacey suggested making the whole process a little simpler. "A strong arm is all that is required."

That was easy for her to say. After ten minutes Lacey's arms felt like they'd been put through an intensive workout at the gym. Things didn't improve when the aunts refused to allow them to use pre-made chocolate chips and instead made them smash up sheets of milk chocolate from Sage's chocolate shop into chunks to mix into the dough. One painfully zested orange later and a Band-Aid on her zested finger, Lacey finally rolled out her dough and transferred it to one of the big industrial fridges. Zac had finished ten minutes before her and stood leaning against his workstation, his bowls and cutlery already rinsed and neatly stacked ready for the dishwasher before him.

"Cutting it a bit fine there."

"Make haste not speed." Lacey put her chin up as she marched past him. "It's the finished product that counts not who finishes first."

"Your dough did look a little gloopy. Ready to pay your fine?"

"At least mine didn't have lumps of butter in."

It was almost unbelievable. Zac Malone smiling, joking, and relaxed. Unbelievable and more than a little dangerous because without that big old keep out sign it was all too hard to stay away. Lacey took a step forward, almost without meaning to, and another until they were almost touching. Almost. "You have flour in your hair," she said, her voice a little hoarse as she reached up and flicked it away.

"Yeah?" He didn't move, still under her touch. "You have flour right here." And his thumb skimmed across the curve of her cheek, setting fire to every nerve he touched. Lacey was paralyzed, aware of nothing but that light fleeting caress, of the dark heat in his eyes as they followed his thumb's progress across her cheek and down to the very corner of her mouth. She swallowed, willing the thumb to keep moving, every atom wanting to know what it would feel like if he ran his thumb across her bottom lip. He stilled, eyes boring into hers, before his hand dropped and he stepped back. "I'll help you clear up."

"Right. Thanks." Lacey stepped back as well. "I'll just...you know... I'll be back in a minute." Her heart was hammering as she walked as fast as she could out of the kitchen and fled into the downstairs bathroom. She stared into the mirror with dismay. Her eyes were bright, her cheeks flushed, and her lips swollen. All that from a caress. "You need to date more," she told herself firmly as she ran the cold faucet until it was as chilled as possible and splashed the icy water on her face. Dating. It was the only answer. Her kind-hearted, homely husband wasn't going to just materialize; she needed to go out and find him.

Only right now he didn't seem as appealing as he used to, and when she closed her eyes and tried to focus on him it was Zac Malone's mocking eyes she saw instead.

THE SUN WAS trying to peek through the low cloud but there was a bitter chill in the air as Zac walked briskly along the river, his gaze fixed firmly on the frozen ground, his hands stuffed into the pockets of his huge, puffy coat. He'd thought the coat overkill when the clerk had suggested it but right now, huddled in it against the sharp wind, he was relieved he'd gone for it even though it seemed fitter for skiing than ambling through town.

What the hell had just happened? One minute he was putting dough in the fridge and the next...

No, no he had to go further back than that. Go back to the moment Lacey Hathaway had widened those big blue eyes and asked him to help with the Bake-Off and he had fallen hook, line, and sinker. It had been fun though, the competitive element, the jokes, the camaraderie between Lacey and himself as the aunts had lectured and instructed. Comfortable—right until the moment she had touched him. Right until the moment he had touched her. That hadn't been comfortable at all.

Her skin was so soft, silky. What would her lips have felt like? So full and tempting...

He increased his pace.

He could, theoretically, ask her out. He was attracted to her and he was pretty sure judging by the way she'd stilled under his touch that she felt the same way. He could take her out for a fancy meal at the fancy hotel on Main Street and kiss her goodnight on her porch.

His hands curled into fists.

He had nothing to offer a girl like Lacey and in a few weeks he'd be gone. Better to take a step back, walk away. Just like he usually did.

Only usually he didn't care either way. This town, that house, that girl were all worming their way into his consciousness, somehow easing their way through his barriers so seamlessly he didn't even realize they were through until he found himself standing in a kitchen, spatula in hand, trying to make a girl smile.

Zac hadn't taken too much notice of his route but to his surprise he looked up to find himself outside the house earmarked for the after-school club if the fundraising was as successful as Lacey hoped it would be. He slowed as he reached the peeling fence, halting at the driveway and looking at the dilapidated front, trying to see it through Lacey's eyes. Cleaned up, done up, and a second home to the town's kids.

He squeezed his eyes shut, the old aches rising once more. How different would things have been if he'd had a place like this as a refuge? No. There was no point dwelling on the past. No point at all. He forced his eyes open and took a deep breath. He was well paid, successful, owned his own business, his own apartment, had insurance, a 401k, his suits were handmade, and his gym fancier than many five-star hotels. He'd shaken the dust of his old town off long ago. There was no reason for him to go back, mentally or physically.

It was just... Zac swallowed. He thought he'd trained himself to want no one, to need no one. But less than a week in Crooked Corner and all that training seemed to be melting away like the chocolate in the cookies he'd baked earlier. He would be gone in five weeks. He couldn't allow anyone to get any closer.

He couldn't allow Lacey to get any closer…

Zac stepped onto the driveway. Maybe he'd take a look around, see if there were any easy fixes he could offer to do while they were waiting for the money to get raised. He'd always enjoyed fixing things up, self-taught at first then working his way through Caltech on a construction crew. There wasn't much scope for fixing things in his sleek, new, glass and chrome apartment.

As he headed to the house he noticed that someone had hung up a hoop up over the garage and the ground in front had been cleared of snow. Zac spied a ball sitting against the fence and, unable to resist, he quickly walked forward and scooped it up. He gave it a tentative bounce and then another before—with a twist of his torso—leaping and neatly putting it through the hoop. Perfect!

He didn't do team sports, hadn't for a long time, and he hadn't had the time or motivation to use the hoop hanging over the garage at home when he'd hit his teens. For a while back then, though, he'd been thought not bad, had had a spot on his elementary school team and hopes of a place on the team when he got to junior high. And then it had all fallen apart. He bounced the ball again, darting from left to right against an imaginary foe before neatly putting it through the hoop once more.

"That's mine." A sullen voice recalled him to his surroundings and Zac turned, the ball still under one arm. A teenage boy stood by the gate, shoulders hunched, his thin jacket no protection against the cold. Recognition flashed in Zac's brain. It was the boy he'd seen his first day here, the boy who reminded him all too clearly of himself. "Sorry," he said easily. "I saw it here and couldn't resist." He held the ball out and the boy stepped forward slowly to retrieve it. "Zac Malone. I'm new in town."

The boy flashed him a glance, which mingled trepidation with a clear *I don't care* attitude. "Whatever."

"It's been a while since I played." The boy clearly couldn't wait to get away but somehow Zac couldn't just turn his back. He'd been like that once: prickly and defensive, quick to show he didn't need anybody and yet all the time desperate for someone to notice, for someone to care. Maybe he'd got it wrong. Maybe this boy had a proper coat somewhere and chose the thin khaki cotton out of defiance. Maybe he had a hoop on a freshly painted garage back home but chose to play here at this deserted, run-down house for kicks—but Zac doubted it. He knew a kindred spirit when he saw one. "Fancy a game?"

"With you?" The cutting glance quite clearly showed that twenty-eight was ancient to thirteen or fourteen and Zac might as well have been in his usual suit and tie for all the credibility this kid gave him.

"I don't see anyone else here. I was just planning on

shooting some hoops then heading to the diner for a burger."
He flashed the boy a conspiratorial grin. "The house where
I'm staying is full of women. I needed some peace." He sent
an apologetic thought Lacey and the aunts' way but he had a
feeling they wouldn't mind, that they'd approve of his
motivation.

The boy just stood there and Zac shifted, awkward in the
silence. What was he doing? A stranger in town making
overtures to a sulky teen could be misconstrued in the worst
way but Zac was damned if he wasn't going to try and see
what was going on. "Unless there's anywhere better? But I
heard the diner's a pretty safe bet."

"They do good burgers there," the boy volunteered.

"Yeah? I tell you what. Humor me and let me shoot
some more hoops with this ball and then I'll buy you a
burger as thanks. Don't worry, I'll sit elsewhere. Wouldn't
want to ruin your street cred."

"I don't have any." The boy's voice was bleak and Zac
felt an answering pull deep in his chest, right where all
memories and feelings were tightly buried.

"Yeah? Me neither, as you'll see when you whup my ass
at basketball. What's your name? I usually like to know the
name of those who are about to defeat me."

"Ty."

"Hi, Ty. Okay, you go first. First to what? Thirty?"

Half an hour later Zac had a warm glow partly from the
exercise and partly from seeing Ty lose some of the kicked-

dog look as they got into the game. Zac discarded the jacket soon after they started and looped it over his arm as they left the house and began to make their way back to Main Street and to the diner.

"Nice coat," Ty said with a nod toward it. "Great for skiing as it's not too heavy and flexible as well."

Zac ached with sympathy at the offhand words. There was his answer. Ty wasn't wearing the inadequate jacket for fashion; he probably had nothing else.

"It's probably a little overkill for walking around Marietta." Zac looked at it ruefully. "I think the sales clerk took one look at me and realized I was an ignorant Californian who knew nothing about snow and talked me into the biggest commission he could."

"California?" Ty's eyes lit up. "Is that where you're from? I'd love to go there, to get the heck out of this small town."

"I grew up in a small town a little like this," Zac said. "Over in Connecticut. Couldn't wait to get out either, only it seems to me that the people are friendlier here. I've been dragged into some kind of fundraising thing for that house we were at earlier. Nobody bothered about things like that where I grew up. They fundraised for nice-to-haves: museums and theaters and things. Not that there's anything wrong with museums and theaters but they didn't care about taking care of their own. I get the feeling that they care here."

Ty didn't answer but he continued to walk alongside Zac

and entered the diner with him, sliding into the same booth. "Have anything you want," Zac told him. "You deserve it. I could say I was out of practice but that would be a mean-spirited excuse. You beat me fair and square."

IT WAS DARK by the time he got back to Crooked Corner. The burger had indeed been very good but far more satisfying had been watching Ty wolf two burgers, a large fries, onion rings, a root beer, and a chocolate milkshake before demolishing a large slice of apple pie.

As he'd expected there had been a few suspicious and surprised glances thrown Zac's way but he had gritted his teeth and introduced himself in a breezy style that reminded him of Lacey. Yes, he was the auditor; no it wouldn't take him long to sort everything out at Town Hall. Yes, he was staying at Crooked Corner and yes, he was entering the Bake-Off for them. No he couldn't cook. That's how he'd come across Ty; he'd gone to take a look at the house. It was a fine project.

His charm offensive had worked and by the time he'd paid the check he'd had several more invitations for coffee and pool games that he'd turned down with his busy schedule as a convenient excuse. Only those invitations didn't feel as intrusive as they usually did.

Lacey was alone in the kitchen, a glass of milk and a plate

of crumbled cookies in front of her. In spite of their best efforts his had been under-baked and raw at the bottom and hers had been so brittle they crumbled at a touch. Aunt Patty had said menacingly that he had better practice until he got it right and Zac didn't get the feeling she was exaggerating.

"Hey." Lacey looked up from the notepad she was scribbling in as he leaned against the doorframe, her smile tentative. "Cookie?"

"No, thanks, I had a burger at Main Street Diner."

"They're good there."

"Why are you in? On a Saturday night?" They weren't the words he had intended to say but they spilled out regardless. It seemed wrong that this vibrant girl was alone in the house with a plate of overcooked cookies and a calico cat to keep her company.

Lacey blinked. "I…I'm a bit of a homebody."

"At what? Twenty-four? Twenty-five? You should be out…" He paused. What did people do in places like this? "At a bar, playing pool, or dancing. Having fun."

"I have cookies," she pointed out. "And I'm working on my interview schedule for the week. Can I interview you on Friday? As advance publicity for the Bake-Off? I'm talking to all the bachelors; you're not the only one."

"Sure," he said and she gazed at him in disbelief. "Really? That's great, thanks, Zac."

He took a step into the room, hooking a chair and easing himself down into it. "I met a kid today. Ty something."

"Ty? About thirteen?" He nodded. "That's probably Ty Evans. He lives with his grandparents on the other side of town."

The frustration burst out of him. "I bought him a burger and the kid ate like he was starving. His jacket is completely inadequate; his shoes were wet through."

Lacey stared at him. "That's odd. I haven't seen him or his grandparents for a while but they are a good family. Are you sure?"

"I know half-starved and neglected when I see it."

"Okay. I'll talk to the aunts and see what they know. They're an old-fashioned family, proud, the kind who won't ask for help. If something is wrong they might be hiding it."

Zac reached out and snagged one of the cookies, breaking it in half and watching the crumbs fall onto the kitchen table. "I know a little about barriers," he said hoarsely. "About how hard it can be to trust people. I want to help."

Lacey put a hand over his. The soft warmth of her touch burrowed deep inside, aching as it thawed him. "You are helping. I know baking a few cookies seems crazy to you but it is a really big deal. And if something is wrong with Ty then you are the first to notice, the first he's allowed to notice, which means you might just be exactly what that kid needs."

Chapter Six

"I DON'T KNOW about you guys but right now tomorrow feels like Christmas and my birthday rolled into one. Sometimes February can feel a little bleak, you know? Especially for those of us who aren't expecting roses and chocolates in two weeks' time. But tomorrow some of Marietta's finest bachelors will be proving that there is more to them than chiseled jaws and come-hither eyes and promising us that it's their skills in the kitchen that will make us swoon."

Lacey took a quick breath, winked at a horrified-looking Zac, and carried on. "But who are these eight brave souls willing to bare their baking skills to our critical taste buds? I'll be chatting to them all over the next two weeks but I'm kicking off with the Crooked Corner's own bachelor: Zac Malone. Hi, Zac."

"Hi."

Lacey suppressed a grin. Zac looked like he was in the dentist's chair, not the comfortable leather desk chair her guests usually sat in. He leaned forward, his elbows on the desk, eyes fixed on the noticeboard she hung schedules, reminders, and notes on. She loved her little booth. It was nothing fancy, less technical than the student radio booth she had occupied for most of her four years at Montana State. She had to share it with the volunteer DJs who kept Radio KMCM going from the five a.m. early slot for early-rising ranchers and farmers to the late-night hosts who put Marietta to bed with a soothing mixture of phone-ins and music.

As station manager and the only paid member of staff, Lacey was in charge of the roster, advertising, and all administration as well as her own show. Although it was a demanding role and not well paid, seen more as a stepping stone than a long-term career, she loved every moment she spent in the small station—and if she managed to recruit an intern or two as she was hoping then her own workload would be a little less onerous.

But much as she enjoyed the juggling of budgets and demands that running the station required it was here in this booth—headphones on, music cued, guest in chair—that she came alive. She might spend more time in her office but the booth was her second home.

"Zac is our very own knight in shining armor," she went on. "My own brother, Nat, was supposed to be our sacrificial bachelor but he couldn't get back to Marietta in time so we're very grateful to Zac for stepping in. Zac is also guiding the good folk at Town Hall to an easier financial life and installing new systems over there so we're doubly grateful to him. So, Zac, how are you finding Marietta?"

"Cold."

"Zac's traveled to us from San Francisco. He's still acclimatizing. Have you always lived in San Francisco, Zac? There's a hint of the Northeast in your accent, am I right?" This was the joy of interviewing; she got to ask questions that in any other situation would be nosy at best, interrogative at worst. Not that asking about where a person grew up was that intrusive but as Zac never volunteered anything about himself Lacey was aware she was taking advantage of her professional position.

"A little. I grew up in Connecticut."

Lacey glanced at him in surprise. He acted like a city boy. Connecticut brought to mind pretty small towns—a little like Marietta. Maybe it wasn't the unfamiliar he disliked about Marietta, maybe it was the all too familiar. "Connecticut?" Not the most intelligent question she'd ever asked.

"It's in New England, just above New York," he said helpfully.

"Thanks for the geography lesson." She tried to ignore his smirk but could feel an answering smile tugging at her lips. "It gets pretty cold in Connecticut though, or have you been in the Bay Area so long you've forgotten what winter really feels like?"

"I've not been back to New England since college," he

confirmed. "Left after graduation and never went back. I like the milder north Californian climate, and I really enjoy the laid-back San Franciscan vibe. Plus I prefer the anonymity of a city. Small-town living can be kind of intense."

"And yet here you are. Not only has it snowed pretty much nonstop since you got here but far from being anonymous you're about to take part in the Bachelor Bake-Off. What brought that about? Apart from my shameless begging and winning ways?"

"I..." Zac paused. The silence expanded. Lacey's first instinct was to rush in and fill the gap but she made herself hold still as Zac visibly wrestled with whatever words were in his head. It wasn't the pause of a man at a loss for words; it was the pause of a man who was going to say something deal-breaking.

"I know what it's like," he said finally. "I know what it's like to be alone. To shoulder responsibilities that you're not old enough for. To not know how to fit in homework alongside taking care of the house and working enough jobs to pay the worst of the bills. To wear clothes that don't quite fit—that aren't quite clean enough. I know this house is for everyone. For all Marietta's kids. And that's how it should be. But there will always be kids who need it more, maybe just for a little while, and I'm in this for them."

Lacey swallowed, aware her eyes were filling with unprofessional tears, her heart aching at the desolate tone she'd heard in Zac's voice. All of the other questions she had prepared for Zac and for the other bachelors now seemed irrelevant. Their favorite cake, baking secrets, their perfect date... All so trivial. "That's inspiring." She winced at the trite words.

"Not really. To be honest I was so focused on getting out and getting on it didn't occur to me that I *could* do anything for kids who found themselves in a similar position, nor that maybe I should. But when you showed me the house I realized it would be selfish to walk away when I know what a difference somewhere like Harry's House can make. That's all. Besides—" he grinned at her "—it appealed to my competitive nature. Not the main Bake-Off. As a complete beginner I'm settling for mid-table mediocrity but I am intending to win the Crooked Corner mini version."

"Glad I could help." Lacey seized the lighter topic he offered her gladly. It wasn't that she hadn't done difficult interviews before or touched on hard topics; she had. It just seemed more personal with Zac and she didn't want to dwell on why that might be. They weren't even friends, not really. She'd hardly seen him all week although she came home each night to the scent of orange and warm chocolate wafting from the kitchen.

"Listeners, you're probably a little confused right now. As some of you know I might live with two culinary geniuses but I haven't been blessed with the Hathaway baking gene. Zac quite correctly pointed out that it seemed wrong for me to expect him to learn to bake in a week if I wasn't willing to try myself. So, to the horror of my aunts, our neighbors, our brave fire crews, and the insurance folk, I am endeavoring to learn to make cookies, a pie, and a cake alongside our bachelor here. Without much tangible success it has to be said. Zac, how are you finding the baking lessons?"

"Terrifying," he admitted.

"Aunt Patty says baking is simple chemistry, which is bad news for those of us who struggled to fill their science requirement in college. Aunt Priscilla says it's simple math. Now, I am a media graduate but you, Zac Malone, own a company which—and I'm reading from the website here—will take care of all your accounting needs, install software that will also take care of all your accounting needs, and audit and train your staff so they are comfortable taking care of your accounting needs. Wow, I didn't realize accounting was so needy. Now, I might be wrong but isn't accounting just math? And if so does that give you a tactical advantage?"

The brown eyes gleamed. "Lacey, I have the greatest respect for your aunts but there is no correlation between a spreadsheet and a perfect bake. And I know this because I have tried."

"Really?"

He nodded. "I have tried project managing every step—weights, timings, position on the baking sheet and in the oven. I've built in all the parameters and probabilities and you know what I realized?" He was leaning close now, his voice soft as if this were private, not being broadcast to whole of Marietta.

"What?"

"That there's nothing scientific about it. It's magic. Your aunts might tell me its chemistry and math but I've seen them just throw ingredients into a bowl: no weighing, no measuring, just mix it up. And yet somehow they turn them into something incredible. Something that I with all my careful measurements and following of instructions haven't been able to replicate. There must be a wand involved somewhere but I just haven't seen it yet."

"Magic? That would explain a lot. So, you even put baking instructions into a spreadsheet. Tell me, Zac, did you always want to be an accountant?"

The gleam in his eye intensified. "Of course. Doesn't every kid? The suit, the car, the spreadsheets…"

"Absolutely. Every child's dream right along with pilot and Batman."

"Maybe there was a brief train driver phase, and some kind of sports star, obviously, the usual American dream. But I knew by the time I left junior high that I wanted a proper job. Security, to work for myself."

"And now you do. Is it how you imagined or do you still have secret dreams of being picked for the Knicks? I mean, if you could be anything, anything at all, would you choose a different path now? Or is it spreadsheets or nothing?"

"I like making things, not cookies but things out of wood. Maybe one day I'll retire to a cabin by a lake and carve chairs and be a hermit. That doesn't sound like a bad way to end up."

Even his retirement dreams involved being alone. Anonymous city living or a hermit by a lake. Zac Malone didn't mean to let anyone in. Lacey just didn't know why that realization made her heart ache. "Thanks, Zac. So there you have it, everyone: our first bachelor. I'll be interviewing the other seven over the next two weeks so stay tuned. And remember the excitement starts tomorrow. Aprons will be donned and spoons flourished at four p.m. at Marietta High. We're starting off with the cookies round and you'll all get a chance to bid for the masterpieces our bakers produce right after the judging.

"If that's not enough to induce you along don't forget we are also holding an amazing raffle and you definitely don't want to miss out on that. The top prize is a night in the honeymoon suite at Graff's and I, for one, am planning on buying as many tickets as I can! There will also be lots of stalls including Sage's amazing chocolates and Jillian Parker has promised to provide something extra special on her jewelry stall with prices for all budgets—so bring your wallets, people! I'll see you there. Here's some Maroon Five with *Sugar* to get you all in the baking spirit and next up we have the local sports roundup with Mitch Holden."

Lacey pulled her headphones off and swiveled round to face Zac. "Thank you, Zac, that was amazing. Thank you for coming along and for being so honest. You went over and above the call of duty. I owe you." That kind of personal touch was radio gold; she knew that all too well.

"It's all for a good cause, right?"

"So that's why you were so cross at the weekend? About Ty?"

The closed look she was beginning to know all too well shuttered Zac's face as he shoved the chair back and jumped to his feet. "I don't want to get into it, Lacey. It's the past. It's dead and buried. Are we done here?"

She looked up at his set face and nodded. "Yep."

"Good, I need some air." Zac strode the short distance to the booth door and opened it before turning back to Lacey. "Coming?"

THEY WALKED IN silence along the pretty Main Street. Cheerful fairy lights still hung on many storefronts reflecting off the snow below. The stores were mostly still open, warm and welcoming as people walked home from work, enticing passersby to pop in and collect things they needed for the weekend. Everyone they passed called out greetings to Lacey. She seemed to be on first-name terms with the entire town. Most of them nodded curiously at Zac, whether they'd heard him on the radio or were wondering what he was doing with Lacey he didn't know but the interest itched away at him.

"Where do you want to go?" Lacey said as they reached

the outskirts of town. "It's a little early to go to Grey's—that's the local bar—but there's the diner if you're hungry or you want a Friday night beer after the trauma of being interviewed by me."

"I don't drink alcohol."

"Oh. Okay." She didn't push it but he could feel the sidelong glance she shot him.

"Go ahead."

"Go ahead what?"

"Ask me why?"

"Zac, lots of people don't drink and besides, it's none of my business."

"And that's ever stopped you before?"

"That's not fair," she protested. "I've been very restrained with you, actually. It's not my fault I have an enquiring mind."

He almost smiled at that. He could practically see the question marks whirling round her brain whenever they were together. He looked around. Inviting as Marietta looked he didn't want to shop and he wasn't hungry. "Let's walk out of town. I know it's dark…"

"It's a Friday. The lake's lit up for ice-skating and it's a pretty walk that way."

Of course it was pretty; everything about this town was pretty. But the thought didn't irritate him the way it would have done a week ago.

The air was cold and sharp, scented with pine and snow

as they headed down the path leading to the lake. It was dimly lit and Zac could make out footsteps, hoof marks and the telltale marks of a sled. A wry smile tipped his mouth. Obviously Marietta ran to horse-drawn sleighs.

"I grew up in a town a little like Marietta," he said abruptly. "Nicely kept, lots of flowers and fresh paint to keep it looking good, locally owned stores, a couple of elementary schools, a good junior high and high school. It was commutable to New York, just, if you didn't mind getting up at dawn and getting back once the kids were in bed—and many fathers didn't. It was mostly the fathers who commuted. The mothers tended to be stay-at-home types—the ones we knew anyway: the Country Club, gym-going, designer-clad types. A new car every other year and a house on the ocean for the summer to make up for never seeing their husbands. I lived in a big house with a dog and a tree house and played Little League and thought that was how the world was."

"It is for many people. It's what I always wanted. Not so much the big house but the dog, the stability."

He couldn't acknowledge her words because if he did he knew he wouldn't be able to carry on. This version of him, this truth had been buried when he headed south and he'd never intended to resurrect it, but the second he'd driven into Marietta memories had begun to stir. The moment he had seen Ty they had awakened like a kraken emerging from the deep. "When I was twelve my dad left. He'd been sleeping with his PA and she was pregnant. He made it clear that his new family took precedence. He sold our house, bought us a much smaller one on the outskirts of town, and moved to New York with his new wife and family. Told my mom she'd have to economize and get a job, that he couldn't afford two households."

"Ouch."

He sighed. "We weren't the first people this happened to; mostly the discarded families moved to start over in a new town. But my mom didn't want to move. Nor did she want to get a job or live in a smaller house in a less classy neighborhood, although there were no really poor neighborhoods in our town. She was so angry, so bitter. And as her pre-divorce social circle consisted of a bunch of snobs who didn't want to associate with bad luck—and liked the women they knew to be safely paired off—she got bitter *and* lonely. She didn't get a job and move on with her life. Instead she drank to forget."

Lacey didn't say anything but a mittened hand slid into his, warm and comforting. Zac grasped it, as if it were a lifeline.

"One Christmas I had the latest sneakers and video games; the next there was nothing under the tree. There *was* no tree. Mom said she couldn't face it. She spent the day in bed. By the time I was thirteen I was cooking for us both—well, heating things up, and trying to hide her credit cards so I could pay the bills and spend the support Dad sent through on food before it went on liquor."

"Didn't you say anything to your dad?"

"He didn't want to hear. I visited him a couple of times but he said it was too disruptive for Vicky and the baby and he'd come and see me, catch a game, grab some dinner. Only he never did. He mailed his check once a month and that was that. He was done with us. And every week my mom checked out more and more. We started to play this game—she'd hide the bottles she bought. I'd find them and pour them away. Only we never talked about it. I never said, hey, Mom, I chucked away the vodka in the linen closet and she never said, hey, Zac, where's my vodka? We just pretended it was normal for her to sit at home all day watching TV, never sorting things around the house or getting a job."

"So you did it all?"

"By fourteen I was working: lawn service, fixing things for neighbors, that kind of thing. Any cash-in-hand job I could do I did. I was doing my best to keep the house from falling apart, to feed us and wash the clothes and keep up with my schoolwork. I knew that was key. I knew if I was ever going to get out I needed to study. By this point she'd graduated from bottles at home to bars. She'd be out all night and sleep all day. We barely communicated unless she was particularly hungover and vicious."

"But you got out?"

"Headed south the day I graduated high school and never looked back. I had a part scholarship at Caltech and spent my summers working construction to make up the rest. This is the furthest north I've been since. I set up the company a couple of years out of college, auditing and recommending software for smaller firms; now we develop our own software, run training sessions, audit entire towns."

The mittened hand squeezed his. "Very impressive. But why, Mr. Boss Man, aren't you in a penthouse smoking cigars and sleeping on a bed of one hundred dollar bills and leaving the actual work to the minions?"

The teasing tone was exactly what he needed to pull him out of the past. He grinned at the visual Lacey's words conjured up. "We're not that big yet, although I'm working on it. We run remotely; we don't really have a big central office so I can manage most situations on the road, even hiring because most of my staff are dotted around the country. It's only the developing arm and essential admin that's based in San Francisco." Besides, he liked being on the road, rootless. Moving from place to place. Too long in his apartment and he started to feel the walls closing in.

"And your mom?"

"Died of a stroke. She was barely fifty. Brought on by alcohol. So, you can see why I don't fancy a beer after a long day."

"I'm so sorry, Zac. Sorry that the people who were supposed to be supporting you failed you like that."

But that wasn't why he was telling her. After all, parents let their kids down all the time in a multitude of ways. "The thing is, that town of mine prided itself on its sense of community. It won awards, was always fundraising for worthy projects. But as soon as we needed them they turned away. No one reached out to my mom, no one but the guys who hung around in bars. No one saw I was hungry or if they did they looked away. Worse, no one saw that I was lonely, that I just needed someone to tell me it was going to be okay. They knew I was dressing out of thrift stores, that I worked three jobs at sixteen, that I dropped all my extra curriculars just so I could get by. And they didn't even offer a friendly word. We were shunned. No more invites to sleepovers or to dinners or camping vacations. My pretty little town turned its back on us."

"It's not like that here."

"Isn't it? I think what you're doing with the house is great, Lacey, I really do. But Ty and his family need help now. You can't wait for him to come to you, because he never will. And the longer he gets left out, the harder it's going to be to let anyone in, ever."

Was he talking about Ty or was he talking about himself? Zac wasn't sure and the last thing he needed was the sympathy shining out of Lacey's eyes. He increased his pace, marching through the snow. Three baking contests, a few more weeks of work, and he could get out of here, no looking back. Return to small cities, big cities, motels, and the anonymity he craved. That was what he wanted, wasn't it? But with Lacey's hand still warm in his, it was hard to remember why.

Chapter Seven

T HE PATH LEADING to the lake had been quiet, just the two of them in an enchanted snowy wood, the way lit by the occasional lantern, the bright winter moon, and the stars; but as they neared the lake Lacey could hear the shouts and laughter of a busy evening's skating. The lake was usually frozen solid over the winter and the people of Marietta took full advantage of the natural rink.

As Lacey and Zac walked around the last bend in the path, the lake opened up before them. Ringed by trees and mountains, with fairy lights threaded through the nearest trees and wooden stalls set up on the nearest bank offering skate hire, hot chocolate, and snacks, the lake was buzzing. Teens in groups of friends or on dates, older children attending their weekly lessons, families with small children holding their parents' hands or pushing penguin skate aids— it seemed that half of Marietta had decided to take advantage of the dry, clear night.

Lacey stopped at the edge of the trees and subtly tugged her hand out of Zac's, not wanting anyone to see them and draw the wrong conclusion. "Do you skate?"

"A little. You?"

"A little." She couldn't keep the wistfulness from her voice. "Traveling around we got to try lots and lots of things for a lesson or two, but we didn't get the chance to do anything properly except music. On a good year we would come back to Grandpop's ranch for Christmas and then we'd come here or skate on the pond outside the house, but I never got the chance to be really good."

"Did you want to be really good?"

"I wanted the glittery costumes and to be able to leap and spin and make people gasp," she admitted feeling a little foolish as she confided her cherished childhood dream. "I don't know if I would have ever got to that level but it's nice to imagine."

"You're musical though?"

Lacey pulled a face. "Proficient. I had to be with my parents and Nat. If you didn't play there wasn't much for you to do. I play the violin and the piano, sing a bit. But I don't do it much, not anymore. Music is meant to make you feel free but music was the reason I never settled down, why I was always dragged from one place to another."

"So you don't use the talents you do have and hanker after the ones you don't?"

"That makes me sound a little pathetic," she said, startled by the harsh assessment. "I wouldn't say I'm madly talented at any instrument. I don't have the passion to move from technically okay to really good but nor do I spend my time oiling skates I'll never use and sewing sequins onto costumes I'll never wear. I love what I do. I'm content with my life."

"Content?" He raised an eyebrow. "Twenty-five is young to settle for content."

"This from a man who spends his life on the run?" As soon as the words left her mouth Lacey knew she had gone too far. She barely knew Zac after all. "I'm sorry, I didn't mean…"

"You did and you're right. But it works for me. Does settling work for you?"

She stared at him, surprised by his clinical assessment. "I haven't settled. I love my job, my home—how is that settling?"

"Sitting in alone on a Saturday night while your great-aunts are out gallivanting, just a cat for company?"

Lacey kicked a piece of snow back and forth. Put like that her life did seem somewhat lacking. "It's a very nice cat." Although Patchwork wasn't even hers; he belonged to Aunt Priscilla.

"You don't want your own place? To work for a bigger network? I know you've seen the world but you might find there's other places that you'd be happy in. Staying still can be just as effective a way to hide as always moving."

"This is all I ever wanted, Zac. To live here, in Marietta, to belong. Why would I give that up? How would I be happier chasing dreams elsewhere?"

"Only you know the answer to that, Lacey." He began to walk again, heading toward the wooden stalls. "That hot chocolate smells good. Want one?"

"Sure." She followed him but his words echoed round and round in her head. She hadn't settled! She chose this life. She liked living with the aunts, loved her room at Crooked Corner in the turret with its window seat and odd hexagonal shape. So what she didn't go out much? She was busy and fulfilled. She didn't have time for anything much outside work and the community affairs she helped with.

The chocolate Zac handed her was hot, rich, and sweet and the comforting taste and smell restored some of Lacey's equilibrium. She leaned against a tree and watched the skate school, kids of around nine and ten earnestly practicing their steps. They all looked adorable with their colorful hats and scarves and mittens and big coats bulking them out so they looked like small roly-poly snow children. She hadn't made it to the lake this year. Hadn't been skating since Nat visited two Christmases ago.

"You want to have a go, don't you?" Zac's voice made her jump and she swallowed the chocolate abruptly, almost scalding her throat.

"A little," she admitted.

"A lot. Why don't you?"

"I don't like skating alone." As soon as she said the words she felt the truth of them and her shiver wasn't just from the cold. "Come on, let's walk back. I told the aunts I'd be home for dinner."

Zac fell into step beside her. It wasn't the comfortable comradeship of the walk to the lake. The air crackled with tension and Lacey knew it was because Zac had made her confront a few unpalatable truths about the life she cherished so much. She *was* lonely. Not unbearably, but she still hadn't quite found her place, her people.

Oh, she had friends; she was friends with the whole town. Top of everyone's list when they needed a favor, a helping hand, someone to man a stall or help behind the scenes at a kids' production or collect Christmas boxes for needy families. She was invited to parties and openings and weddings. If she bumped into any one of a myriad people they'd suggest a coffee or lunch.

But she didn't have anyone who really got her. No one, apart from the aunts, to confide in, to really laugh with. She didn't have a group to meet up with at Grey's to play pool with or gossip with. She belonged to a book group at the library and was on a couple of committees and that was pretty much her social whirl. Her great-aunts, on the other hand, seemed to be out every other night.

Nor did she really date. Not because she wasn't interested in meeting someone or because she was too busy but because her relationships rarely progressed beyond a few dates, hardly ever past the coffee or a movie stage. Sometimes she thought she was fated to always be the outsider looking in at a world she yearned to be part of. Not that anyone knew. She hid her loneliness with her work and her laughter and a nonstop stream of conversation and a microphone and camera. She interviewed people, she told their stories, but somehow, where it mattered most, she didn't connect with them.

But things seemed different with Zac; *she* was different. Her chest tightened. She'd worked so hard to make a life here and in less than two weeks Zac Malone had pulled back the curtain and shown it up for the illusion it was.

Zac slowed his pace. "You're surprisingly quiet. You okay?"

"Yes, of course." She covered the truth up with a smile and a light tone, just like she always did. "Just hungry. I think it's pot roast tonight. I'm hoping for Aunt Patty's patented creamed potatoes and her fried green beans to go with it. You haven't lived until you've tried her green beans. I don't know what she does to them but they are ambrosial."

"You don't have to pretend, Lacey, not with me."

She couldn't look at him. "Yes, I do. Especially with you."

"Why?"

"Because you make me nervous. Because you challenge me; you make me think." She shook her head in frustration. "I don't know why. I hardly know you…"

His laugh was short. "I think you know me better than anyone else alive."

The truth of his words hit her hard and she stopped.

"Maybe it's because we're both lonely. That's all this is."

"This?"

"This connection." She looked up at him. He was half shadowed in the moonlight, the silvery light making him seem otherworldly. "There is a connection, isn't there? I'm not imagining it?"

"Beyond being equally bad at baking?" He blew out a long breath, digging his hands into his pockets. "Yes. There's something."

"It scares me," she said honestly. "I know what I want, what I'm looking for, and I don't know how you fit in."

"I don't. I'm just passing through."

Lacey stared up at the hooded gaze. It would be so easy to reach up and touch him. So easy to stand on her tiptoes, to lean in, to kiss him. What would his kiss be like? Hard and demanding? Tender? Sweet and sensual?

But what then? He said it himself. He was just passing through. What good would getting any closer do? All it would achieve would be too remind her of what she was missing.

"Stop looking at me like that," Zac said hoarsely.

"Like what?"

"Like you're Little Red Riding Hood and I'm the big bad wolf."

She took a step back. "Hey, if I'm anything I'm the woodcutter."

A smile tugged at his mouth. "Is that right?"

"You'd better believe it."

"Oh I do," he assured her. "If you wanted to, I think you'd be quite capable of felling any wolf."

Lacey's mouth was dry, her heart hammering so loudly it seemed to reverberate off the trees. "Zac, I don't casually date."

He stilled. "No?"

"No. I'm not good at getting close to people, not without my camera or a microphone or an activity. I don't know what to say or how to be when it's just me."

"You seem to do just fine from what I can see."

"Maybe that's because you're not going to stay. You're safe. If you find me lacking in any way it doesn't matter because you were never going to be a long-term prospect anyway."

"I don't find you lacking." The softness in his voice sent trembles down her spine and she took another step back to safety.

"I don't want to get hurt. I don't want you to hurt me. I don't know how to play these games."

"I didn't know we were playing games."

"But that's all we could ever do because you don't want what I do."

"What do you want, Lacey?"

"I want the life I didn't have. Stability. I want a house on a nice street with a swing in the yard and an attic stuffed full of boxes of seasonal decorations that we use year after year. I want wipe-clean walls so it doesn't matter if the kids make a mess. I want a dog, from a rescue somewhere, a dog that isn't much to look at and is somewhat of a mutt but has loads of character. And I want kids. Kids who know every inch of their neighborhood and have memories around every corner."

"I won't stop you having any of that. We've only known each other two weeks and I'll be out of here before winter's through."

He was right. It was just two weeks and yet if felt far longer. "If I knew how to flirt and just have fun then maybe things would be different. But I don't. If we...if we take this connection any further, then it might be too hard for me when you walk out of my life. I know it sounds ridiculous, on two weeks' acquaintance, but you deserve to know the truth. You deserve to know why I really, really want you to kiss me right now and why I really, really can't."

"You're overthinking this."

"Maybe. But that's how I feel."

A smile softened his face. "Message received loud and clear. Come on, woodcutter. Escort this wolf safely through the wood."

SOMEHOW OVER THE last week, Zac had lost the habit of eating quietly in his room. The aunts set a place at the kitchen table for him, always the same place, with the same cheerful, polka dot crockery, a neatly rolled napkin, and a tall glass with etched leaves on it. Somehow Zac had got into the habit of clearing the table, rinsing the dishes, and stacking the dishwasher. Almost as if he were one of the family. Usually Lacey helped, talking incessantly or dancing round the kitchen to the radio—set to Radio KMCM of course—singing along in her rich, tuneful voice.

But tonight she had been quiet through dinner and excused herself as soon as Zac began to clear. He couldn't blame her. He hadn't been able to give her the reassurances she had wanted, the reassurances she had needed, and now she knew she was safer keeping her distance from him. It was probably for the best.

He turned the hot water faucet on and let it run to scalding. Truth was he admired her for being so clear about what she wanted. For calling out the tension that had been slowly building between them and letting him know she wanted no part of it. She was right. If she was the kind of girl who was happy with a brief flirtation, maybe a fling, then they could have acted on the attraction between them.

But Lacey Hathaway wasn't that kind of girl. She wasn't the kind of girl to settle for anything short of her dreams. But really. What were the men of Marietta thinking? Why weren't they forming an orderly line around the block desperate to win her heart? If he was the kind of man capable of wooing and winning a girl like Lacey he would make darned sure he was at the front of that line.

There should be a line.

Over the last week he hadn't returned to his room to work. Instead he had retreated into the aunts' second kitchen, instructions and measurements and spreadsheets in hand to practice making the cookies, but tonight he had no appetite for the rich smell of baking cookie dough. Tomorrow he would be the focus of attention. People would be watching him, judging him, and just because it was all in fun and for a good cause didn't make it any easier.

The sound of a piano drifted into the kitchen. Someone was picking out a tune, hesitantly at first then slowly with more confidence. After five minutes or so the bass line began to add depth. He didn't recognize the jaunty music although the folk elements to it made him suspect it was probably one of Lacey's parents' original numbers. Zac still hadn't visited any room in the rambling old Victorian except the kitchens or his own quarters despite a standing invite to come and join the family any time he wanted, but the piano pulled him along the corridor and into the den, which sat directly off the hallway at the front of the house.

It was a warm cozy room, a fire leaping in the grate, books lining one wall and a welcoming window seat overlooking the front lawn, drapes pulled to keep out the chilly night sky. The piano was on the far wall, an antique-looking affair in a rich cherry wood, the keys yellow with age and slightly dented with use. Lacey sat on the stool, head bowed as she worked her way through the tune. Zac pulled a second stool over and sat down next to her, watching her fingers as they flew over the keys, deftly pulling music out of the old instrument.

"You're pretty good," he said as she finally lifted her hands, pushing back the silky blonde hair that had fallen over her face as she played.

"I'm out of practice. Dad would be really disappointed. But I just don't have the time to spend an hour a day keeping up—or any real reason to."

"Don't you want to play for fun? There must be loads of amateur bands round here. I'm sure they'd snap you up."

Lacey pressed the middle C, the rich tone echoing around the room, before walking her fingers up the keyboard in a rapid scale. "Amateur? In my family it's professional or not at all. Which means not at all for me. I haven't played in public since I was fifteen. Mom and Dad used to love to make us come on and sing backing vocals, or Nat would play his guitar and I'd do the fiddle refrain. He loved it, obviously; I always wanted to be back in the hotel doing my homework or in the crowd photographing it—not being center stage."

"But you're center stage when you're on the radio or if you're putting a documentary together. You're planning to film yourself tomorrow morning when we have our mini bake-off aren't you? How's that different?"

She blew a frustrated breath. "I don't know but it is.

Mom and Dad would say playing music is just telling a story, like putting a documentary together or writing an article. I don't mind my work being out there for all to see and judge but I just hate singing or playing in public. I know that I spend three hours a day talking to all of Marietta but it's different to standing on a stage. Less revealing."

Zac looked down at her long, graceful fingers still caressing the keys. "Lacey. Can we be friends? I don't have many, and that's been fine with me. But I like you, I like your company, and I'd hate to think that our moment of honesty by the lake has spoiled that. I agree, dating is a bad idea. But friendship would be nice. If you'll have me."

She crashed a discordant chord and then another. "You want to be friends? Is that something people decide or something that just is?"

"I don't know. I told you I don't have many and that's an exaggeration. I think my college roommate counts me as a friend; he's a persistent type. I get on well with a few of my colleagues and there's a couple of guys I play racquetball with…"

"A veritable Jay Gatsby."

"Maybe I am. He didn't really have anyone did he? Not when the music stopped." The emptiness inside shocked him. He had chosen this path, preferred it. But right now the safe way felt very much like a cop-out. A cop-out from life and the opportunities it offered.

Lacey slid a glance his way. "So what will it entail? Being

friends? Braiding each other's hair and talking about boys?"

"You can try and braid my hair if it makes you happy." Zac ran a hand through his close-cropped hair with a grin. "I'll pass if that's okay. I never was good with the knots in Scouts. But we could talk about boys if you want. In fact let's do that."

"You want to talk about boys?" Lacey swiveled round on her stool and fixed him with an incredulous glare.

"More about men than boys," he conceded, enjoying her surprise. "Bachelors to be specific."

Pushing her stool back Lacey jumped to her feet. "I need chocolate," she said. "Possibly strong coffee."

"You said it yourself, Lacey. You want the house, the dog, the kids. Now it's the twenty-first century, you're a hardworking talented woman, I'm sure you're more than capable of providing that home for yourself but if you were thinking of the more traditional family route you missed out one essential ingredient. A husband or life partner."

"I am *not* having this conversation with you."

"I'm just being honest like a good friend should. Now I am about to meet seven of Marietta's most eligible men. Why don't I find out if any of them seem a good match for you? I could put in a good word."

"I do not need fixing up!"

"It's Friday night and here you are. At home. Even the cat's gone out."

"Because I have a busy day tomorrow."

"And last Friday night? The one before?"

Lacey pursed her lips. "I don't see that that's any of your business."

"We're friends aren't we?" Zac said silkily. "That makes it my business. Look, I'll do a deal with you. We never did decide what the penalty would be if I win the mini bake-off. You win and I do a day of small-town activities of your choice: milkshakes, sleigh rides, skating—bring it all on. But if I win I get to set you up on a date."

"Why?" Lacey threw her hands up in frustration. "Why would you want to do that? What does it matter to you?"

"I'm a nomad, Lacey, and that's the way I like it. But there was a moment down by that lake when I wished I wasn't. Just a moment when I wanted to be the kind of man it would be safe for you to kiss. The kind of man who would be worthy of that kiss. I'm not but I'd like to know that he was out there somewhere. The guy who will make you happy. The guy who can take you skating."

Lacey didn't answer for a long moment, her lashes veiling her eyes. Her cheeks flushed as she stood in the middle of the room, hands twisted together. "Okay."

"Okay?" Her capitulation wasn't quite as sweet as it should have been because somewhere deep and primal Zac wasn't at all keen on the idea of Lacey dating anyone at all. He squashed his inner caveman down and smiled. "Trust me, I'll pick the perfect guy."

"*If* you win."

"I have spreadsheets," he reminded her. "I don't think my win is in any doubt at all."

Chapter Eight

L ACEY HOISTED THE small video camera onto her shoulder and threaded her way through the crowd. The hall at Marietta High School was heaving as people lined up for tea, coffee and other refreshments or shopped at the stalls set up along one wall, all selling a variety of enticing goods.

Jillian Parker's jewelry store seemed to be particularly popular with couples, Lacey noted. Of course Valentine's Day was just around the corner. Her parents always sent her a card, her aunts made little heart-shaped cakes, and there was usually a gift from Patchwork but that was it. No mystery admirers, not bouquets, no silver hearts with a message inscribed. Still, it wasn't all bad; at least Patchwork had good taste. Last year the cat had bought some of Lacey's favorite praline chocolate from Sage's shop.

As she wandered through the crowd various people gave her a smile and a wave and Lacey acknowledged them back. She stopped to quickly chat with a slender blonde in a colorful shirt. She'd interviewed Noelle Olsen recently about her new dance studio and had promised to try out an adult ballet class. Somehow she'd never had time. She should make time.

"Hey, Lacey, loved this morning's webcast." Jane wove her way through the crowd to greet her. How the slim brunette had the energy to coordinate a project like this and raise her gorgeous toddler twins Lacey had no idea, but the woman seemed to have endless energy and enthusiasm. Like Lacey she was a newcomer to Marietta. More so, she didn't have family here going back generations like Lacey did, and yet somehow she'd found a place right in the heart of the town. Jane had heaps of good friends and was now happily married to her rancher husband, Sam. He used to be a loner, Lacey remembered, watching him smile at his wife across the room, a twin's hand held firmly in each of his. Look at him now. People did change…

She dragged her mind back to the matter at hand. "Thanks, Jane. I could have done without dropping the flour and forgetting to put the oven on. I don't know where my head was."

"Somewhere on the other side of the kitchen with that glorious bachelor of yours?" Jane suggested with a grin. "I am more than satisfied with my gorgeous husband but Zac has cheekbones that could cut butter. No wonder your mind kept drifting. We could have done with the webcam drifting a little bit more too—tip for next week. Think about the ratings, Lacey!"

"It's not like that." Lacey's cheeks heated up at the

knowing smile on the other woman's face. "We're just friends, that's all. Besides, he's just passing through."

"That's a shame; he's obviously a good person as well as easy on the eye. After all, he doesn't have to be here baking away on his weekend."

"No, I'm very grateful to him. I'd better get over to the kitchen, Jane. I promised to film the baking and judging and do a follow-up webcast tomorrow. I want to get some interviews in with the other contestants too while they bake. I'll get them all to do vox pops when they come in for their radio interviews but the more personal I can make the footage the more hits we get and hopefully that will mean more donations."

"A combination of baking disasters and gorgeous single men sounds like a winning formula to me. It will really put this fundraiser on the map. Thanks, Lacey."

As Lacey made her way into the school cafeteria she saw the judges already chatting and made a mental note to interview them all later. They were a formidable quartet: Sage Carrigan's chocolates were famous statewide and no tourist left Marietta unconverted to her creamy smooth chocolate and inventive palate. Meanwhile Rachel Vaughn owned and ran the Copper Mountain Gingerbread and Dessert Company. Not even the birth of her daughter a year ago had slowed her down.

There was a friendly rivalry between the Copper Mountain Gingerbread and Dessert Company and Crooked

Corner Cakes but as the aunts neither wanted to nor had the facilities to expand beyond the specialty cakes and ranch batch baking they currently offered, it was more good-natured teasing—and a sharing of recipes and skills—than anything more serious. In fact several of the apprentices they trained from time to time had gone on to work for Rachel, but Lacey knew her great-aunts were still keen that Zac do them justice as Rachel would be judging their entrant.

Ryan Henderson was hardly less intimidating. He had trained in Paris as a pastry chef. Lacey spared a moment to pity the poor bachelors faced with such experienced and demanding judges. Hopefully Langdon Hale, the new Fire Chief, would be easier to please!

The competition had already formally started and the eight apron-clad men were at their stations mixing, melting, grating, and stirring. The smells were incredible: hot butter, melting chocolate, vanilla, orange, candied nuts all melding together in a mouthwatering combination—although Lacey knew all too well how quickly the aromatic smell could turn acrid. How she'd managed to burn her cookies after forgetting to turn her oven on she had no idea. One nil to Zac in the mini bake-off stakes. Which meant she had just two weeks to get out of this ridiculous date...

She panned the camera around the cafeteria as the reality of last night's agreement hit her. Was Zac serious? Did he really want to set her up on a date out of what, some kind of altruistic friend thing? Or to make up for walking into her life, turning it upside down whilst knowing he was just going to waltz right on out again? Okay, he was right when he pointed out she wasn't having much success setting herself up but did she really trust him to find her someone compatible? And did she really want to date a man who wasn't Zac?

No. She wasn't going to think about this right now. She had work to do. Lacey walked over to the first workstation where Tyler Carter was gritting his teeth as he mixed his dough, looking like he'd much prefer to be at the gym he owned—or in fact anywhere but in this room. Ingredients were scattered and spilled all around and Lacey had a pang of empathy. She might be no gym goer but it rather looked that where baking was concerned they were right bang on the same page. "Hey, Tyler," she said cheerily. "What are you making?"

He looked up, swiping an arm across his forehead as he did so, leaving flour in his hair. "Chocolate chip cookies—at least that's the idea."

"My favorite."

"I doubt these will be," he almost growled. "I haven't been able to get them right in a single practice session yet."

"I know how that feels. Good luck anyway."

Tyler grunted in acknowledgement as Lacey snagged a chocolate chip from his table and moved on to the next bachelor, Matthew West the town vet. He treated Patchwork so Lacey was already on good terms with him and spent a couple of minutes filming him as he competently mixed up his chocolate macadamia nut cookies. Lacey had heard that he'd been spending some time with Carolyn Hanson who had recently returned to Marietta after working as a chef in New York. It looked like it was time well spent. Matthew seemed calm and unhurried as he melted the chocolate, his neat workstation a stark contrast to many around him.

It was fun moving from bake to bake, chatting with the stressed-looking men, sneaking samples where she could, getting loads of great footage she could use for all kinds of promotional material. It was particularly lovely to see Harry's family, hovering around Avery Wainwright's table. The popular family had elected to sponsor the bachelor through their grocery store and were here to support him. Avery's family were good friends with the Monroes and it was touching that the injured rodeo rider had agreed to use his unexpected downtime to represent them.

Lacey swallowed a lump as she watched Mrs. Monroe, sadness never too far behind her smile. The tragedy was still so raw for her and yet the Monroes pulled together as a family, working their way past the tragedy as a team. It was an all too real reminder why Harry's House was so important, a way of healing wounds as well as providing for the future. Lacey made a mental note to see if she could get Harry's mom and siblings to talk to her for a future webcast, maybe up at the house. It could make some powerful footage.

She'd been to every table bar one. It wasn't that she had

deliberately kept Zac till last, or that she was ignoring him, but she had already got lots of footage of him practicing. It was undeniable that her heart began to beat a little more rapidly as she neared him, her hands slippery on the camera. He was frowning at his dough, the dark eyes narrowed, tense lines around his mouth.

"Hey."

He didn't look up. "I don't understand it. My dough was perfect this morning. Look at this!" He pushed the gloopy mixture with a spoon.

"Add more flour?" Lacey suggested. "Or some milk?"

"You do know they do different things?" The smile that accompanied his words speeded her heartbeat up even more.

"Do they?"

"How's the interviewing going?" Zac lowered his voice. "Any bachelors catching your eye?"

Lacey hastily switched the record function off her camera. "I don't know! I was working, remember?" How could he sound so calm and interested? Last night he'd looked at her mouth as if it was the most delicious thing he'd ever seen and now he was calmly asking if she wanted to date any one of a number of other men. Had she imagined it, the way he'd looked at her? Was it her own attraction to him making her attribute feelings to him he simply didn't have?

"I haven't had a chance to really chat to any of them yet," Zac continued. "But that Jake guy seems nice. Public defender so he has a good job. Not that money's everything but it can make things easier. Raising kids is expensive you know."

"Shush." Lacey knew her cheeks were bright red; they felt on fire. She looked around, thankful nobody was near enough to hear him, and then glared at him. Zac grinned unrepentantly, a mischievous glint in his eyes. "Concentrate on your cookies, Malone. It looks to me like they need all the help you can give them."

"What do you think my chances are?" he asked as he attempted to roll out the sticky mess. Despite the unappetizing look of his cookie mixture plenty of people were passing by his table and noting down his number for the auction. Plenty of women, Lacey noticed. It must be the baker and not the goods attracting their attention.

"Of winning? I don't know, Matthew West looks pretty professional over there." Lacey watched Zac attempt to cut out the first twelve cookies, squinting as he placed them on the first baking sheet. If she looked sideways she could kind of see that they were meant to be stars. "And that guy over there, Wes St. Claire? They are pretty tasty-looking snickerdoodles he's got going on there. How well do you take losing?"

"You're suggesting I may not win?"

"I am preparing you for the possibility…"

Zac looked down at the sheet of unbaked cookies as the mixture spread out, losing the carefully cut out shape they were supposed to be holding. "Fair enough. I won this morning; that will do me for now."

"Zac?" Aunt Priscilla bustled up to the counter, her bright hair falling out of its bun, her lipstick extra bright. Her pink sweatshirt was emblazoned with *Sugar, spice, and all things nice* picked out in rhinestones. It had been Lacey's Christmas present to her. "How is it… Oh." She stared at the gloopy mess, dismay clear on her face. "Why don't you…"

"No coaching, Aunt P," Lacey admonished her. "You don't want him disqualified for cheating."

"No, of course not." Her aunt's innocent look did not fool Lacey for one moment; she knew her all too well. "I would never think of suggesting to Zac that he adds flour before he rolls out the next batch and cuts them, nor that if he sprinkles that sheet of disintegrating stars with a dusting of flour and reshapes them with a blunt knife they may well hold their shape. Not at all."

"Aunt Priscilla! I am going to take you to the refreshment stall and buy you a coffee before you get Zac into serious trouble. We'll see you later, Zac. Good luck—I think you need it!"

"AT LEAST YOU didn't come last." Aunt Patty set a coffee in front of Zac and pulled out a chair for herself. "Where *did* you come exactly?"

"Second to last," Lacey piped up cheerfully from the counter where she sat, swinging her long legs like an overgrown schoolgirl. She waved the snickerdoodle she had bought in the auction at him. "These are delicious. Wes definitely deserved to come second. But, get this, Aunt Patty, Zac's cookies bought in the most at auction. Those girls from Town Hall sure like to keep on the right side of their accountant." The smile she flashed him was only a little mocking.

"I'm sure they tasted better than they looked," Aunt Priscilla said loyally and Zac buried his face in his hands dramatically.

"I let you both down. I'm sorry. I don't know what got into me." That wasn't exactly true. He had a sneaking suspicion he knew exactly why the cookies—which had worked perfectly well this morning—had gone so disastrously wrong in the afternoon.

The other bachelors.

Zac had gone to Marietta High filled with determination to do the right thing and find Lacey a decent date. And any of the other bachelors would fit that bill. They were obviously good guys—look at the effort they were putting on for charity. That was a good sign. All around the right age, had their own teeth and hair as far as he could tell; not one of them seemed like a bum. He could probably pick any name out of a hat and stand back and watch Lacey fall in love.

Trouble was he didn't want Lacey to fall in love. Not

with another guy.

But she couldn't, shouldn't fall in love with him. Which made him feel like the worst kind of heel. He'd watched her making her way around the kitchen, stopping, smiling, chatting, sneaking bits of cookie dough, making the other bachelors laugh. And he'd been seized with some kind of primal possessiveness he didn't even know he owned. He'd wanted to march over and stand there glowering until every other man in the room backed away, until they were a respectful distance away. Until he claimed her as his.

Which was ridiculous. He might be out of practice at this friendship lark but he was pretty sure territorial prowling wasn't how it worked.

No wonder his mind hadn't been on the cookies.

"Don't look so annoyed, Zac; you'll do better next time." Aunt Patty gave his shoulder a reassuring squeeze. "One bad bake does not make a bad baker. I'm sure we can teach you to make a most credible pie."

He looked up at the elegant older woman. "Next time?" He'd been so focused on those damn cookies he'd forgotten there would be a next time. This Bake-Off experience wasn't over, not nearly over.

And if he had trouble with cookies how on earth was he going to manage a whole pie?

"Pie week." Lacey had a dreamy expression on her face. "I do love pie."

"Good thing as you'll be making it right along with me,"

Zac said grinning as the dreamy expression was wiped away as if it had never been, replaced with the same horror of dawning realization he'd felt just a few moments before.

"But pie is hard! Unless, oh! We could always use one of those precooked pie crusts and just fill it…"

"Lacey Anne Hathaway! There'll be no talk of precooked pie crusts in this house. What would your great-grandmother say?" Aunt Patty glared across at her unrepentant niece.

"The real question…" Aunt Priscilla said, reaching over to snag a snickerdoodle from the bag Lacey had brought home. She sniffed it and broke off a piece to sample. "Mmm, these aren't bad."

"The real question is?" Lacey reminded her.

Aunt Priscilla swallowed her bite, her eyes a little glazed with sugar overload. "Hmmm? Oh, yes. The real question is what pie."

"Lemon meringue? Ooh Boston crème? Pumpkin? I do love pumpkin pie…" Lacey had reverted to pie dreamland again.

"Those are all challenging pies," Aunt Patty said cautiously.

"I think we are better sticking to a simple pie crust dough," Aunt Priscilla agreed.

Zac thought about the sticky mess of cookie dough and briefly closed his eyes. Why had he allowed Lacey to talk him into this? He'd lost every evening of the last week to cookie practice and look where that had got him—second to last.

And now pie. He doubted anything about pie crust dough would be simple. "Is there a pie that doesn't involve pastry?" he asked. "Like a sweet version of a shepherd's pie."

"That sounds disgusting," Lacey chimed in as both Ms. Hathaways shook their heads.

"It has to have pastry, Zac."

"Pastry and a filling. But what filling?"

"An apple pie is a classic for a reason."

"Maybe *too* classic. Will it stand out? Some of these boys can bake. This snickerdoodle is very credible."

"How about a chilled pie? Banoffee?"

"Will there be time for a chilled pie? Besides a warm pie straight from the oven attacks all the senses, visually appealing, that enticing smell…"

"You're right. A twist on a classic? Some kind of spice in the pastry? Cinnamon? Ground ginger?"

"Ginger could be interesting. Teamed with what if not apple? Rhubarb?"

"Peaches?"

"Blackberry!"

"Hmmm, tricky. Can be a soggy fruit. And so tart."

"Not if he blind-bakes the pastry and adds the precooked blackberries. He can add sugar to taste then. Maybe with a maple syrup. Maple, ginger, and blackberry. That could work."

"Lattice top? Or no! A ginger-crumble topping. Ideally he should make the ginger snaps during the Bake-Off but that might add an extra layer of complexity."

"Unless it's a traditional crumble topping and not a cookie one?"

Zac realized his head had been snapping between the two older women like a spectator at a tennis match. "Um," he said. "Do I get a say?"

Both women swiveled round to look at him, identical expressions of surprise on their faces. Zac very much suspected they had forgotten his presence. "Of course."

"Absolutely."

Not that he actually had anything to contribute. "Blackberry and ginger sounds fine." He wasn't entirely sure on the flavor combination but he fully accepted this wasn't his area of expertise. "I don't know what blind-baking is but as long as it doesn't involve a blindfold I'm happy to learn and I'd rather not add any extra complexity to the pie after today's less than successful session. So I'm saying a firm no to ginger snaps."

Aunt Patty nodded. "Probably wise, then blackberry ginger crumble pie it is."

"On that note I'd better get to work." Lacey slid gracefully off the counter. "I want to look at today's footage and make six mini segments, one for each day leading up to the next Bake-Off. I'm going to get some one-to-one interviews too, when the guys come in to the radio station, and the Monroes have agreed to speak to me this week over at the house so I should have enough to put a really decent full-length piece together as well as all the fundraising shorts."

"That's very good, dear." Aunt Priscilla beamed up at her niece. "What will you do with it?"

"I'll probably run a screening here in town when the house is ready to be opened but it'll go up online next week before the final Bake-Off so anyone can see it. If they make a donation afterward, all the better. What I really need is to talk to some possible beneficiaries about why it's important, but it's a bit tricky getting the right permissions and I feel a bit awkward approaching kids. There'll be a way. I just need to think it through further."

"I'm sure you'll come up with a solution."

"That reminds me…" Lacey paused at the kitchen door. "Have either of you seen much of the Evanses lately? Harold and Celia Evans? Only Zac met Ty the other day and was a little concerned. I thought it was just teen stuff, you know; he hasn't had the most stable of starts. I could understand a kid like him kicking off a little at small-town life. But I didn't see Harold or Celia at the school today and that's not like them at all. I know Celia used to be a regular at your Quilting Circle, Aunt Priscilla. Have you seen her lately?"

"Not for a while." Priscilla Hathaway's face scrunched with concentration. "She stopped quilting a few years ago; she said her hands weren't what they used to be. But now you mention it she hasn't been to Women's Guild meetings for a while. And I haven't seen much of Harold. He *was* volunteering at the library, I know, but I don't recall seeing him for the last few months. I'll look into it, Lacey."

"Thanks, Aunt P." Her eyes met Zac's for one brief moment and then, with a quick smile around the room, she was gone. All at once the warm, welcoming kitchen felt empty, like the light had gone out of it. While the aunts continued to bicker amiably about the exact proportion of blackberries to syrup to ginger—a fight that looked like it was about to play out in a pie-making contest of their own—Zac slipped out of the room and headed to his own suite of rooms. But now they didn't feel like a welcome sanctuary; they were a reminder that he was a temporary guest here and that Crooked Corner could never be his home. That should be a welcome relief, so why was his chest so heavy at the thought of packing up and moving on?

Chapter Nine

"LACEY, WHERE ARE you off to?" Aunt Patty fixed her with a stern look and Lacey froze in place like a child with one hand in the cookie jar.

"Work…"

"It's Sunday."

"The show must go on, Aunt P, even on a Sunday. Not my show admittedly but I was just going to pop in and…"

"You're popping nowhere. Pie practice day. Remember?"

Of course Lacey remembered. That was why she was up so horrendously early and creeping out of the door. And she intended to keep creeping out of doors till the Bake-Off was well and truly over. After all, if she was too busy to compete then Zac would have to call their ridiculous bet off. Wouldn't he?

Which meant no going on dates she really didn't want to go on. Which meant no watching Zac try and fix her up with another guy. There was of course the whisper of a chance that she would win the next two contests and beat him but the odds weren't good enough to risk it.

"I know and I really wish I could hang around but…"

"We're going to the ranch."

"The ranch?" That changed everything. "Why?"

"Because that was where my mother, your great-grandmother, made the world's best pies. What better place to learn about pastry?"

Lacey swiveled around. "I haven't seen Grandma and Grandpops since Christmas…"

"Exactly. Get yourself ready and then come meet me in the kitchen. I had a baking spree last night and I need help loading the car."

It took less than an hour to get everyone up, fed, dressed, and the car loaded up with coats, snow boots, several boxes of baking, and the ingredients they needed for the day's lesson. There was some tussle about driving. Zac seemed to think that he had a male prerogative to drive and it was true he had the fanciest car. But, as the three women all pointed out, he wasn't used to the roads or the snow and they all were.

They then proceeded to work out who had priority: Patty because she had grown up on the ranch, Priscilla who had lived there most of her adult life or Lacey who, as she tactfully said, was the only one of the three who didn't need glasses to drive. She was soon shouted down and relegated into the back seat with Zac while Aunt Priscilla triumphantly claimed the driving seat.

"Don't get me wrong, I love a road trip, but where are

we going?" Zac could never look unkempt but he was as close to it as Lacey had seen. Faint shadows around his eyes hinted at a less than perfect night's sleep and he hadn't shaved. Lacey had an almost irresistible urge to reach out and run her hand along the bristles. She shoved her hand firmly under her thigh just to make sure she didn't unconsciously act on the urge.

"The ranch."

"That I know, what I don't know is which ranch—why or where. Your aunts gave me fifteen minutes to get ready and told me not to dress like a city boy."

Lacey ran her eyes appreciatively over the cashmere sweater, dark jeans, and freshly polished boots. "I don't think you have much choice," she told him. "No one would mistake you for a cowboy even in thick fog at midnight." She had pulled out her most well-worn, faded jeans and teamed them with a blue tee, a padded check shirt, and her thickest jacket. She wore cowboy boots but had slung her snow boots in the trunk just in case they had an opportunity to get out for a walk. Or, even better, an afternoon's skiing.

"Thanks. I think." He leaned back, a grin crinkling the corner of his eyes. Lacey took a deep breath, all too aware of his proximity in the confined space of the car. His arm lay across the back of the seat as he lounged in his corner, his hand so close it wouldn't take much to lean into his caress. His long legs were corralled in, thighs close enough to touch.

Lacey swallowed, her mouth dry, her body tingling in

every inch of her that could feasibly touch him if the car curved around the mountain bends. She gripped her seat tightly, wedging herself firmly in the corner. Looking up she saw Aunt Priscilla's eyes in the rearview mirror watching her with a knowing look and she shifted awkwardly to stare fixedly out of the window.

"We're going to see my grandparents and my aunt and uncle and cousins."

"The Waltons?"

"No, the Hathaways."

"But they all live together? Like the Waltons?"

"More like the Ewings minus the intrigue, back stabbing, adultery, and shower dreams. My grandma, grandpop, Uncle Walter, Aunt Valerie, and Tilly who's the only cousin at home. She's seventeen. Ted and Will are at college—they're twins—and Fliss, the oldest—she's my age—is in Europe."

"Big family."

"Yep. I loved coming to Three Pines Ranch so much when I was a kid. Fliss and I get on great. I could just step straight into my family and know I was home. I had my own bedroom at the ranch and everything."

"So why not live there when you came to Marietta? Not that your aunts aren't amazing hostesses of course," he added hurriedly, half an eye on the front seat.

Lacey shifted back round so she was facing Zac, careful to keep a good distance between them. Friends was good; she wholeheartedly approved of the idea. It was just her body hadn't got the memo yet and kept tingling at awkward times. "I love the ranch but it's kind of isolated. I wanted to make friends and socialize more and that's hard to do when you're ten miles out of town and halfway up a mountain. But the ranch, it's something else. Surrounded by mountains, nothing around but trees and lakes and fresh air. It's the best medicine in the world."

"Sounds about as different to San Francisco as a place can be."

Lacey tensed as she processed the offhand comment. Somehow over the last week Zac's presence had become so normal she kept forgetting he had a home elsewhere. Not just a home but a place he was in a hurry to return to. That his stay in Marietta was for work only and the second that work was done he'd be gone. Would want to be gone. It was an unwelcome reminder she couldn't afford to get too close, that his friendship offer was a short-term deal.

"I can't imagine living in a big city when there's all this wildness to enjoy. I know I live in town but just five minutes' walk and you can be by the lake or in a forest or start to walk up a mountain." She pulled at her ponytail. "I guess it's in my blood as well as in my heart. My great great-grandfather settled here at the end of the nineteenth century, hacked a living on the mountainside, and won his claim."

"But your parents left before you were born, didn't they?"

"Yes, Nat was born in Marietta—the lucky thing—but I

was born in Vermont. Which is a lovely place but I still think Mom could have planned it better and come home in time. I'm the only Hathaway not to have been born in Marietta for four generations." Not that she was bitter about it. "My great great-grandmother was a mail-order bride, came out west on the mail train to marry a man she didn't know. She was quite a lot younger than he was. I always wondered if they were happy..." Her voice trailed off as she imagined her ancestor getting off the train in the middle of the wilderness, traveling over rough-hewn roads to Marietta and her stranger of a suitor.

"They were," Aunt Patty chimed in from the front. "Grandmother always said the angels must have been guiding her when she answered that advert. He was twenty years older than her but he worshipped her. She nearly died giving birth to my father, and of course a rancher needed sons, plenty of them, but he would never allow her to try for any more children. He said she was more precious than any land could ever be."

Lacey couldn't help a little sigh of longing. What must it be like to be loved like that? Lacey had seen photos of course—Crooked Corner was filled with them—but she had never really thought of the mutton-chopped, severe-looking man and the demure woman as being the hero and heroine of their very own love story. "That's wonderful. That they found each other."

"That's the Hathaway way. We don't fall in love easily

but when we do it's deep and it's forever." Aunt Patty sounded wistful, and Lacey remembered whispers of a tragedy before her great-aunt had moved to Paris and embarked on her career as a model. Was that why she had never married despite being linked to any number of men including several rock stars and, if you believed the gossip, an Italian prince? Lacey had never quite dared ask her aunt. Warm and caring as she was there were clear Keep Out signs around anything too personal, but she liked to believe in the Italian prince.

"Look at your great-grandfather," Aunt Priscilla chimed in. "He was well over thirty when he went to Europe in the war, still unmarried even though half the girls in Marietta were crazy about him. His father had passed on by then and his poor mother was left managing the ranch by herself. But he returned from Europe, safe and sound, with his Scottish war bride and they were very happy for over fifty years."

"They died within a few weeks of each other. It was as if they couldn't bear to carry on without the other. It was hard to be too sad, knowing they were together forever after such a full life. Three children, two grandchildren, six great-grandchildren. That's not a bad legacy," Lacey explained to Zac. It was the kind of legacy she had always dreamed of, and yet it seemed further away than ever.

"Bill brought me back to Three Pines straight after we were married," Aunt Priscilla said. "I wasn't sure about living with his family so far out. I was Marietta born and bred, not a ranch girl. And it wasn't common, in the late sixties, to move in with your in-laws, all my friends had neat little houses in town. And there were so many people to adjust to sharing the house with. Patty of course, and your grandfather and grandmother were already married, Lacey. Your dad was about five and Walter only three. But the whole family made me so welcome it felt like home straight away. It will always be home in some ways but when Bill died I couldn't face being reminded of him in every room. Luckily my aunt left me Crooked Corner and Patty had decided to return home from Paris..."

"I was ready for a change but heading back to the ranch was a little too much of a change after Paris. Marietta suits me fine. I need something urban about me," Aunt Patty threw in.

"I always wished Mom and Dad had stayed on the ranch and I could have grown up surrounded by you all," Lacey said. "I loved coming back for those few weeks every summer but my favorite time was when we could come to you for Thanksgiving or for Christmas, to be part of such a big family for a few days, to have my own room and my own chores. There are no chores when you spend your life in hotel rooms living on room service. All I wanted was some home cooking and someone to tell me to clear the table afterward."

"And that's why we're coming to Three Pines for Zac's pie lesson," Aunt Patty said. "Great pies have been made in this kitchen by generations of women. There's no better place to learn the art of pastry than at the marble slab where my grandmother and mother rolled out pie after pie."

Lacey winked at Zac. "It's just the honor of the entire family on your shoulders, Zac, but no pressure. No pressure at all."

Aunt Priscilla was a careful but speedy driver and despite the windy roads and the ice it was less than half an hour before the car was climbing up the narrow mountain pass that led to Three Pines Ranch. The snow-covered mountains soared into the sky on every side, the white startling against the clear blue. Three Pines was nestled on a large shelf that ran over several mountains and across several thousand acres. The entrance to Hathaway land was marked by the three tall pines that gave the ranch its name. Zac took a deep breath. This was a step beyond a dinner at a friend or date's house. A step beyond eating his dinner with the Hathaway women in the kitchen at Crooked Corner. A step beyond getting pulled into the town's fundraising efforts.

This was allowing himself to be enveloped by a family. Stepping right into the heart of it, a place he hadn't been for a really long time. He'd spent so long never looking back, never allowing himself to miss what he had once had he'd never allowed himself to consider it might, just might, be a part of his future. His heart ached. Hope was dangerous. It just led to bitter disappointment all over again.

This wasn't his place or his family. He belonged on the

road. He had no family. The last time he'd heard from his father was… No, he couldn't remember. His half brother must be sixteen now. Did their father take him to ball games and make sure he didn't shoulder responsibilities he was nowhere near ready for? Or had he moved on to yet another new family, discarding the old as easily as he had discarded Zac and his mom?

Zac shifted in his seat and stared out of the window, barely hearing Lacey as she pointed out landmarks and various places where she, her brother, and cousins had got into one kind of trouble or another. Long, snow-covered fields stretched out on either side of the road, ending only where another mountain soared into the distant heavens. It was magnificent in the winter; he could only imagine how idyllic it must be in the height of summer.

"Look, there it is. Three Pines." Lacey was practically bouncing in her seat as she pointed the house out to him.

It was a large house, although that was probably as well with three generations under one roof. A long, two-storied white wooden house, with a veranda running the whole length of the building, it looked home-like despite its size, the freshness of the green trim and matching shutters and the round windows high under the roof adding to its charm.

Several barns were arranged around a courtyard at one side, a short walk away from the house, on the other side a circular driveway occupied the space before the ranch garages, which were painted to match the house. Aunt Patty pulled the car up neatly in front of the first garage and switched off the engine.

Zac hung back as the women piled out of the car with the confident happiness of people returning home. He didn't like making small talk, and besides, what could he contribute unless they wanted to chat about finance? He knew nothing about ranching or cows. He could barely ride a horse. There had never been a reason to learn.

He jumped as Lacey tucked an arm through his, the touch as comforting as it was oddly welcome. "Come on," she said. "We'll unpack the car later. Grandpops and Grandma are really looking forward to meeting you."

The huge two-story-high hallway only held five people—Lacey's grandparents, aunt and uncle and cousin, and two—no, three—large dogs—but it felt much more crowded there was so much exclaiming, hugging, and laughing, the dogs adding their own contribution to the hubbub. Zac found himself the recipient of two very firm handshakes, two warm hugs, and a self-conscious smile from the teen girl who fell upon Lacey with relief and an exhortation for a private chat at some point that afternoon. While the aunts and the rest of the family went out to unpack the car Lacey and her grandfather ushered Zac into the bright, airy kitchen where bowls, saucepans, scales, and spoons had already been set out.

"Ingredients for three?" Lacey counted the bowls out loud. "One, two, three... Who else is joining us?"

"I believe Tilly is helping your aunts fix the final recipe.

She's a talented baker that one for all her nose studs and hair dye."

"Beaten by a seventeen-year-old." Lacey picked up a handwritten list and stared at it dejectedly. "Look, she's done three different combinations of ingredients for us to try. How did this skip me? I got the Hathaway eyes and hips; I should have got the baking gene too. Come on, Zac, let's wash and apron up."

"Let the man have a drink first," Lacey's grandad interjected. "And an opportunity to look around. Do you like horses, Zac?"

"Drink yes, look around not yet," Lacey said before Zac had an opportunity to frame a diplomatic answer that he probably liked horses just fine; he just had never had an opportunity to get to know any. "I'm really hoping we'll get a chance to ski a little and it gets dark far too early still. I don't want to waste any time."

"Don't be too polite, Zac." Her grandfather fixed Lacey with a glare but Zac could see the love and affection underpinning it. "I know how forceful those three are. I can believe they pushed you into this baking malarkey but don't let them drive you too hard."

"I didn't push him," Lacey protested. "At least, only a little…"

"Oh, she manipulated me all right," Zac said with a grin. "But only because I let her."

"Good man, that's the way to manage a Hathaway woman. Let them have their head and think they've always got their own way. Lacey is the most headstrong of the pack. You're a brave man to take her on."

"It's not like that, Grandpops, we're just friends." Lacey's cheeks were scarlet.

"Just friends, eh? As if I didn't have eyes in my head." And Lacey's grandfather left the kitchen chuckling to himself while Zac did his best to avoid Lacey's eye.

"Pass me that recipe list, then." Baking was always a safe topic of conversation. And far better to concentrate on ingredients and utensils than to notice how particularly blue Lacey's eyes looked while she was wearing that sweater. And far better to think about pastry than to wonder what it would be like to have grown up as part of a family like this. And much *much* better to worry about the ratio of ginger to sugar than to dwell on the knowledge that the lucky man Lacey did settle down with would get to be part of this family.

He just hoped that whomever she picked was deserving. Because he needed to be pretty damn special. The kind of man who would fit in in a place like this. Not the kind of man who had no idea how to be part of a family, the kind who didn't fit in. Not the kind of man who was better off alone.

Chapter Ten

"IF YOU HAVE any preferences on which bachelor you want you'd better tell me," Zac murmured as the aunts prowled around the kitchen table looking at the finished pies and whispering to each other. Tilly's pie had come out perfectly, her crumble neat, her pastry a gorgeous golden brown, but Zac was secretly rather pleased with his effort. Making pie crust pastry was a much more tactile experience than the drudgery of mixing the cookie dough and he'd rather enjoyed feeling it all come together under his fingertips.

He would still have to practice every night and already had planned a few tweaks to the ratio of ginger and syrup but this time, distractions aside, he was confident he could do a lot better than second to last.

Lacey on the other hand had found pie even more of a challenge than cookies and it showed, in both her disgruntled running commentary and in the results. Her pastry was burnt, her crumble topping raw and her blackberry filling both tart and runny. It was a good thing she was prepared to laugh at herself, taking a picture of the aunts' disgusted faces as they tried her filling. She immediately posted it to the fundraising site. "I have a week," she said coolly. "Don't count your chickens yet, Mr. Malone."

"I'm just using basic probability theory. No chickens in my calculations."

"Come and try the pies. We'd be interested to know what you think about the flavorings," Aunt Patty announced and the assorted Hathaways surged forward, plates and forks at the ready. Zac took a few steps back and watched as plates were loaded, pie sampled, and opinions expressed in varying degrees of forcefulness.

"The crust needs more ginger."

"Less ginger. It's too strong."

"I think the crumble topping is too fussy."

"No, no, it's perfect. Looks attractive too."

"Did you say there was maple syrup in these blackberries? I can't taste it."

"The maple is lovely and fresh. It makes the blackberries sing."

Outside of work—and yesterday's Bake-Off—Zac couldn't remember the last time he had been in such close proximity to so many people. Even in this large and airy room it was discombobulating—so many voices, so many opinions, and Lacey right in the middle of the hubbub. "Uncle Walter! It isn't that bad. I'd like to see you do better. I challenge you to make a pie. Next time I'll do a middle-aged rancher Bake-Off and sign you straight up!"

The noise escalated as the family laughed and Walter loudly accepted the challenge. Zac's ears rang as the walls began to close in. His chest tightened and he took another step back, slipping out of the kitchen and into the hallway. He leaned thankfully against the wall enjoying the peace. The hallway was so big, so high that it could easily have been a sterile imposing space but the large vases of winter berries, the warm colors on the walls, and the low velvet couch all softened the effect. The double-width staircase ran up one side to connect with a gallery overhead, which ran round three sides of the space, with corridors branching off on either side to match the corridors on the first floor.

Although there were shared family spaces like the kitchen and a formal sitting room and dining room, Lacey had told him that each family also had their own quarters with bedrooms, baths, offices, and living rooms. Still. Zac couldn't imagine living with so many other people no matter how many private spaces he had.

The ranch was also home to several full-time ranch hands, some of whom lived in a bunkhouse behind the barns and a couple with their families in small houses dotted over the ranch. With the nearest town ten miles of windy roads away the inhabitants of Three Pines were dependent on each other for company and entertainment. It had to get claustrophobic. But the people back in the kitchen didn't seem to feel that way. Under the laughter and bickering even Zac recognized the ties of blood and affection. Ties his mother and father had squandered. He leaned against the staircase post, his throat thick.

"There you are. Did we scare you off? The family gets a little too passionate about food, especially pie, and as you could see everyone has an opinion and likes to express it as loudly and forcefully as possible. It's a little intimidating for new folk. But the good news is you nearly beat Tilly in the taste test, which bodes well for Saturday. Where pastry's concerned she's reckoned to have inherited our Scottish great-grandmother's touch."

"I didn't mean to be rude but I was a little warm." Zac couldn't tell Lacey how he really felt. How it wasn't the heat that drove him out, it was the loneliness. How being around a family like hers just drove home everything he didn't have. It was such weakness. And to be really honest with someone, to allow her all the way in, would just make it harder when he was alone once again. So much safer all around to skate over the truth.

Lacey's eyes scanned his face anxiously and Zac could sense she didn't quite believe him but she didn't push the matter; instead she pushed a strand of silken hair off her face and smiled. "Interesting you should have been too warm. As it happens, I have the perfect remedy…"

"ARE YOU SURE you know how to drive this thing?"

"Better than you, I'll bet," Lacey flung over her shoulder. "Hold tight, city boy."

The city boy tag was a little unfair. Zac looked like a true Montana Man in Nat's gray ski trousers and red and gray jacket, shades masking his dark eyes. It was a good thing that Nat, like Lacey, still had a room in the small wing at the end of the house that had traditionally been theirs whenever her parents had a break from touring—and that he stored both his summer riding gear and winter ski outfits in his closet there. The men were of a height and a shoe size although Zac was a shade slimmer than her brother.

Lacey released the throttle and the snowmobile edged forward across the field. She kept it at a sedate pace until she was safely past the barns and the skittish horses and onto the snow-covered path, and then upped the speed until they were flying along, snow dancing in the air as the treads dislodged it. The ice-filled air was bracing on her face and she could feel her ponytail bouncing along in rhythm with the snowmobile. "You okay back there?"

"Less talk more concentrating," Zac called back and Lacey laughed, upping the speed a little more as she did so.

"Relax, Zac, I've been driving one of these since I was twelve."

"Somehow that doesn't make me feel better."

Lacey ignored him and continued to edge the speed up. The buildings had disappeared behind them and the lower slopes of the mountain were beginning to tower over them as Lacey headed away from the plains and toward the nearest of the majestic mountains that surrounded Three Pines. After a few minutes a small wooden building came into view and Lacey headed for it, sweeping the snowmobile round in a stylish circle as she pulled up outside it. The hut was positioned at the bottom of a gentle slope, which gradually steepened as it rose.

"There it is, nursery slopes for the first few hundred yards and something a little more challenging if you are prepared to climb up to it. We used to beg Grandpops to put in a lift but he just laughed at us and told us we'd never be real cowboys if we were too weak to walk up a hill. So it's our own legs or nothing." She paused, stricken by a sudden thought. "Do you ski? I didn't think to ask. We do have sledges if you don't."

"Ski? Is that what we're doing? No I don't. Is that a problem?"

Lacey stared, apologies and offers of lessons on her lips when Zac continued deadpan. "I snowboard though. Does that help?"

She swatted him. "Ha, ha. I didn't think there would be much opportunity in San Francisco and as you actively avoid the snow…"

"I prefer to surf but there are mountains near enough to drive to for a day's powder," he admitted and a picture of a wetsuit-clad Zac, hair wet, surfboard under one arm, crept into Lacey's mind and refused to be dislodged no matter how much she told herself it was inappropriate. Especially as the top of the wetsuit was unzipped, drops of seawater glistening on his bare chest.

Lacey dragged her mind back to reality and the matter at hand. "Great. We have several snowboards. Come and choose."

She fished the hut key out of her pocket and opened the door. Thanks to the solar panels on the roof the hut was equipped with electricity. She flipped the light switch and with some satisfaction heard Zac's intake of breath as the rows of skis, snowboards, boots, and poles were illuminated. A small kitchen area stood to the right of the door, just a sink, a kettle, a microwave, and some instant hot chocolate and tins of soup. At the far end a door led into a shower and washroom.

"This is very complete." Zac rubbed his eyes as he stared around. "I've seen less well equipped hire centers."

A glow of pride stole through Lacey at the impressed tone in his voice. "When Uncle Bill was alive and Aunt Patty came back for Christmas there could be as many as fifteen of us out here on a good day. It made sense to keep the equipment here and have facilities to heat small, chilly folk up with hot chocolate and marshmallows. We always headed here Christmas Eve after church and Christmas Day after presents and before the cooking began.

"It gets used at other times of course. Any of the ranch

hands who want can use it and the twins are very keen skiers; they head out here almost every day when they're home, but skiing is a really big part of our Christmas and it feels so special to have our own slopes. Not that it will be like this forever—this personal—if Fliss, my cousin, has her way. She wants us to expand into tourism, riding vacations in summer, skiing in winter, opening up more slopes for winter sports. Build log cabins, offer the authentic cowboy experience. That kind of thing."

"You don't like the idea?"

"I don't live here. I don't intend to run Three Pines and I doubt I could even if I wanted to. I spent every summer here but I didn't grow up with it the way my cousins did. Ranching isn't a job easily learned; it has to be absorbed. And it makes sense. I guess I'm just a little selfish. This is ours; these slopes are ours. I don't like the idea of sharing them."

And yet she'd brought Zac here.

"Come on, snowboards are over there. Second to the top of the slope makes the winner a hot chocolate."

Thanks to the sun and the sheltered aspect of the slopes it was warm work climbing to the optimum starting point but that didn't stop them taking several turns. Zac was a natural snowboarder, light on his feet with a stylish turn that Lacey envied. She knew she had good balance and was capable of tackling any slope no matter the gradient but she didn't look quite as at home as Zac with his casual grace and almost instinctive feel for the snow. "Are you sure you just take the odd day-trip to the mountains?" she asked suspiciously after watching him execute a perfect turn. "Or are you a secret competitive snowboarder?"

"Occasionally I've taken part in an amateur tournament," he confessed. "But I don't have time to snowboard often, I promise."

"You're wasted on these slopes, much as I love them. If we get a chance I'll drive you out to the nearest resort—there are a few slopes nearby with different levels of difficulty and, you'll be glad to hear, real ski lifts. Obviously you're a little busy over the next two weeks. Maybe the week after."

"If I'm still here. I initially contracted to be here six weeks to two months but everything is running much more smoothly than I anticipated. There's a chance I might be able to wrap it up in five weeks, even though I've lost my evenings to baking practice."

"Oh, of course. Well, if you're still here then." Lacey didn't want to speculate why her chest tightened at Zac's words. His presence was only temporary; she knew that. But it was so easy to forget.

She cast an experienced eye at the sky. "We have time for one more go. Do you want to snowboard again or do you like to sledge? No, don't tell me, you've competed in the downhill bobsleigh at the Olympics but only when you had some spare time?"

Zac laughed. "No, I couldn't tell you the last time I went

on a sledge. Certainly not since I was a kid but I'm willing to give it a go."

"Race?" Lacey suggested. Surely this was one competition she could win. He had weight on his side but tall as she was she was more compact than him, more experienced, and had been sledging down these slopes since she was a toddler. Not that she was at all competitive.

"Of course, what's the penalty? You already owe me three hot chocolates."

"Double or nothing."

"I'm not sure I can drink six hot chocolates," Zac said dryly. "Okay, you win and your debt is canceled and I owe you the richest hot chocolate Marietta has to offer. I win and you owe me a penalty of my choice."

Lacey's heart missed a beat. She couldn't see Zac's expression behind the darkened ski visor but there was an undercurrent to his voice she didn't quite understand, something rich and dark and dangerous.

But she was going to win this so what was the harm? "Done."

"Shake on it?"

Lacey hesitated then slipped her hand out of its bulky padded glove and extended it to Zac. His grip was warm, firm, and Lacey had an urge to fall into it, to be enfolded by him. She pulled her hand free, quickly, pasting a bright smile on her face. "Sledges are this way. They're all named so take your pick but Rudolph is mine. You can't miss it; it has a red nose painted on."

After ten or so trudges up to the top of the slopes, Lacey's calves and thighs were beginning to ache. Not only did the slope get quite a bit sleeper the higher she got but cutting a path through the snow was challenging even after they had trodden a visible path. The sledge was heavy as she tugged it behind her, her breath coming quick and her body uncomfortably warm in its thermal layers. She welcomed every twinge. Welcomed any physical pain that took her mind away from thinking about the dark undercurrents in Zac's voice, the feel of his hand encompassing hers.

Was she a fool to spend time alone with him knowing how thin the line was between friendship and attraction? Knowing how short a time he would be in her life? Zac was right. She should be exploring all the dating opportunities she had in Marietta and the surrounding counties. There were entire ranches full of men. Men who held the same values she did, who wanted the same things. She should be taking them skiing not a restless traveler, eager for the next town, the next adventure.

"Okay. Who's counting us down?" They'd reached the top of the slope and Zac had already positioned his sledge, concentration writ clear on his face. Lacey lined hers up a good thirty feet away and sat down, gripping the rope tightly between her hands. She stared down the slope, mentally plotting the best route, not just for speed but also as bump free as possible and hopefully one that would keep her clear out of Zac's path.

"I will. Are you ready?"

"Oh yes."

Lacey shot him a quick glance. Zac sounded determined; he was as keen to win this as she was. "Okay then…" She put one leg up onto the sledge, ready, the other poised to push. "Ready. Get set. Go!" With the last word she pushed with her leg and then again as the sledge moved sluggishly through the snow. A third push and it gained traction, moving faster and faster. Lacey pulled her second leg in, bracing both against the metal bar, the rope in her hands and her body leaning forward to add as much weight as possible.

It was like flying, the sledge skimming over the snow at breakneck speed, the wind rushing in her ears as snow flew up in a fine spray, coating her in a mist. She yelled in exhalation and heard Zac echo the call.

All her attention was on the route ahead, on keeping her course, ensuring her weight was distributed properly, that she was as streamlined as she could be as she plummeted down the slope. She hit the more gentle lower slopes, momentum keeping her going until an unseen bump lurched her to one side. Lacey hung on, tugging at the rope to get back on track, shifting her weight to ensure she didn't fall. She desperately tried to get back into position without losing speed.

She'd lost sight of Zac until a warning yell made her look up and she saw him hurtling toward her, pulling his rope to try and change direction. Lacey closed her eyes as he skimmed closer, closer and then, with just a slight clip of her rail he was upon her. The clip knocked her to one side and she tumbled into the snow, rolling over and over until she finally came to a stop.

Lacey blinked the snow out of her eyes and tentatively tried to sit, a few twinges warning her of impending bruises. Snow covered her arms and legs as if she had been coated in it and she shook it off, sitting up gingerly.

"Lacey? Are you okay?" Zac appeared beside her. "I tried to avoid you but I was going so fast…"

"It's fine. I'm fine. It was just a clip. My fault, I was so busy trying to win I didn't get out of the way in time. Are you okay?"

"Yes, I didn't fall. Are you hurt? Anything sprained, bruised, or broken?"

"Only my pride," she said ruefully. "Honestly. What a klutz." She took the hand he held out to her and allowed Zac to haul her to her feet. She stamped her feet to dislodge the snow. "Look, nothing broken."

"Good." Zac had pushed his visor up and as Lacey looked up, a quip ready to break the tension, she faltered. His gaze was intent, heat darkening his eyes. Zac reached out and tucked a piece of hair behind her ear. "I thought I'd hurt you."

"You didn't," she almost whispered. "And I knew what I was getting into all along."

"Did you?"

Lacey knew he wasn't talking about sledging anymore. "I think so."

"I wish I knew."

His gaze was searching and Lacey's mouth dried as she desperately tried to remember all the reasons kissing Zac Malone was a bad idea. There were many, *many* reasons. She'd listed them to herself before going to sleep last night and the night before but standing here in front of him, within touching distance, her mind was a blank. All she could think of was how impossibly warm brown eyes could be, how much she wanted to trace the line of his cheek, how firm his mouth was.

And then he stepped back. "Your family will be worrying about us. We'd better get back. Are you up to driving the snowmobile or shall I?"

Lacey blinked, as if waking up from a dream, suddenly aware that snow had got in to the neck of her jacket and her boots and she was rapidly chilling. "I'm fine," she said, more tartly than she meant to and she stepped forward to retrieve her sledge, wobbling on sore legs as she did so. A warm hand covered hers as Zac gently took the rope out of her unresisting grasp.

"I'll take these back down."

"Fine," she said aware that she was repeating herself and, after one more pat down, Lacey began to make her way down the slope and toward the small hut, her mind whirling in endless circles. Why had he backed away? Because she'd asked him to? She should be glad that Zac was adhering to her rules. But Lacey couldn't help reliving that moment when she'd thought he was going to kiss her over and over. And not one of the many excellent reasons for not getting involved with Zac seemed worth the disappointment that had stabbed through her when he'd stepped away.

It was cowardice—she knew that—fear of being rejected that stopped her getting close to people. She spent her life hiding behind a wall of chat and helpfulness, yet remaining the eternal outsider. Zac had felt safe; he was leaving after all. But there had been nothing safe in his gaze then.

Maybe she should be taking some chances. Otherwise what? She'd stay at Crooked Corner all her life? Turn forty and still be living with her great-aunts like some Victorian spinster? Rejection was part of life and if she continued to let the fear of it rule her then she would never achieve anything including the family, the stability she craved so much.

And maybe, just maybe she should start with Zac. So he was leaving. Did that mean they couldn't explore what was between them just for a little while? Or would the fallout be more than her inexperienced heart could handle?

Chapter Eleven

L ACEY WAS UNUSUALLY quiet. She'd disappeared to her cousin's room once they got back to the ranch house and had barely spoken on the ride home, staring out of the window instead. She'd wanted him to kiss her out on the ski slope, Zac knew that with every fiber of his being. And oh how he had wanted to.

But he'd made her a promise just a few nights ago. He'd promised to be her friend. He'd promised not to hurt her. A few kisses on a few weeks' acquaintance wouldn't normally present any kind of problem but Lacey wasn't a love them and leave them kind of girl. Her heart was too big, too open, too vulnerable. But still, Zac noticed the shadow in her eyes and hated himself for putting it there.

The sound of the piano floated through the house, something mournful, the perfect soundtrack to Zac's mood. He grabbed his coat. There was only one way to make amends.

When he returned to Crooked Corner fifteen minutes later Lacey was still at the piano, the sad refrain clearly audible as Zac walked up the porch steps. He stamped the snow off his shoes before opening the front door. Instead of heading down the hall to his rooms he took a sharp left into the den. Lacey was bent over the piano, intent on the notes spilling from her rapidly moving fingers. He stood there for a moment, drinking her in. The hastily knotted blonde hair, wisps caressing her long neck, the curve of her back, her supple waist. She was like coming home.

Zac shook the thought from his head, stepping forward abruptly. "I sabotaged your toboggan win so here, consider it an apology and your victory spoils in one."

Lacey's hands paused on the keys as she looked up at his words. Her eyes widened as, with a flourish, Zac presented her with the large paper cup. "Double chocolate, cream, chocolate sauce, and marshmallows. Oh and sprinkles."

"Oh my goodness," she breathed taking the cup from him reverentially, inhaling the rich aroma blissfully. "This is amazing."

"Sage was about to shut up shop but I persuaded her this was an emergency."

"You didn't have to."

"If you don't want it, I'm sure I can find a home for it…"

"No!" Lacey clutched the cup protectively. "I want it. Touch it at your peril."

Zac shrugged his coat off and sank onto the loveseat in the window bay, warmth spreading through him as she smiled at him. "Your peril I should think; I'm not sure I

JESSICA GILMORE

could manage that much chocolate and cream without being ill."

"That's because you're an amateur. You have to build up to a hot chocolate like this. Years of practice."

"I believe you." He paused, searching for the right words. "Lacey. Thank you for today. For letting me meet your family."

Her gaze dropped to the bright cup, lashes long and thick on the curve of her cheek. "Thank the aunts, it was their idea."

"They took their cue from you. I haven't spent a day as part of a family for a really long time. If the aunts had given me a choice I'd have run a marathon rather than go but in the end I enjoyed it."

"They liked you. You're welcome there any time, you know."

"Your grandfather said—it was nice of him. I like him; I like them all."

"They're likeable people."

Zac picked up a photo from the side table and studied it. It was a picture of Lacey in her college graduation gown, flanked by three beaming people who could only be her parents and brother. Their love and pride for her shone in every wide smile. "Lacey, can I ask you something?"

She looked at him, eyes wary. "Of course."

"I get why you love Marietta so much. I get it's the community you always wanted. And yes, as small towns go…"

Her lush mouth curved into a smile. "Yes? As small towns go?"

"It's an okay place to spend a few weeks," he conceded. "Maybe longer for many folk. But, Lacey, you *have* a community; you have a great family who love you, who are always there if you need them. There will always be a place for you at Three Pines, a room just for you, with your name on the door."

"My grandma embroidered that nameplate when I was born. I can't take it off the door; it would break her heart."

"Hey." He held his hands up. "I like unicorns, no judging here. But that's what I mean, you belong there, you always will no matter where you go or what you do, no matter which cousin takes over eventually. You could turn up in fifty years and they would take you in and give you a home. That's pretty special. Pretty unique."

"I guess."

"I just wonder why that doesn't make you want to spread your wings a bit. You have so much to offer. Running Radio KMCM can't challenge you, not really. And where can you go from here? The breakfast show *and* drive time?"

"You think I have to travel to be challenged? Live in a big city, commute, practice hot yoga, eat tuna sashimi, and drink skinny soy flat whites to be a success?"

Zac grinned at the scorn in her voice. "Steady on, you have just described my last three ex-girlfriends, and no. I'm not saying you need to be a millennial *Sex and the City* clone at all. What I am saying is that there are many bigger radio stations where you would have more reach, be more challenged, would get more opportunities. Are you really content to spend your life doing drive time in Marietta? In twenty years are you going to look back and wish you'd tried something else, something more? Moved outside your comfort zone a little?"

Lacey took a sip of the hot chocolate, closing her eyes briefly as she did so. "That's amazing, thank you, Zac." She took another and then set the cup on top of the piano. "Why does it matter what I do? You said it yourself. You'll be gone in a month, we probably won't ever see each other again. Why do you care how I'll feel when I'm forty?"

"I don't know," he admitted. "But I do." Something cracked in his chest at the words. It had been so long since he'd cared about anything or anyone. "If I thought you were really happy…"

"How would you know whether I'm happy or not? We don't know each other at all."

"Is that really what you think?"

She held his gaze for a long moment and then her eyes dropped. "No. I suppose not."

"Hey. You're the one who said you'd settled for content, remember? I'm just wondering why. If I had a family like yours, with the freedom and support to reach for happiness, I don't think I'd settle at all…"

Lacey rolled her shoulders, pulling her hair out of its elastic as she did so. It fell in soft waves around her face, spilling over her shoulders like a glorious cloak. Zac's hands curled into fists, the urge to reach out and touch was almost too much for him. She sighed, reaching for the hot chocolate and inhaling before she spoke again.

"There're a few family characteristics. Most, although not all, Hathaways bake, you know that. It's said we only fall in love once and when we do it's for life, like swans. None of my generation have met anyone yet so I don't know how true that is but it certainly seems to be that way for my dad, my grandparents, my uncles and aunts. And some of us are wanderers. Dad, Aunt Patty, Fliss, Nat. They all have itchy feet and with it the gift of being instantly at home anywhere and with anyone. You should see Nat. He can walk into a bar in a strange town and by the end of the night he's met several kindred spirits and made lifelong friends. But the rest of us are homebodies, a little more reticent. I'm a homebody. It was never that easy for me."

She took a sip and stared across the room. "It wasn't as hard when I was in elementary school. Kids of that age tend to be curious and welcoming. I'd usually find myself the center of attention, guest of honor at parties, invited on sleepovers. I was always desolate when we moved on and I had to say goodbye, unkept promises of friends for life every time, but I soon settled again. But once I reached junior high it all changed. People have their tribes at that age; they don't want to include a newcomer, not straight away, and we were never anywhere long enough for me to find my niche.

"I got used to being alone but I never liked it. I begged my parents to let me live at Three Pines or send me to boarding school but they couldn't understand why I didn't enjoy traveling like Nat did. When I came to live with the aunts everything changed. I had a place. I belonged to Crooked Corner. And if I'd lost the knack of easily making friends, if I never did quite work out where I belonged, it was okay because I was at school for two whole years. I could be in the play, work on the school radio, join student council, organize yearbook."

"You became a doer."

"I guess so. Always surrounded by people, always needed. It meant I never felt lonely. I always had a place even if I didn't have a tribe of my own. I still do. When I'm on the radio I have hundreds of friends, thousands. I'm part of something."

"And that's enough?"

"I'm safe here, Zac. There's nothing wrong with wanting to be safe."

"No. I suppose not. Not unless it stops you being the best you can be, stops you achieving all you can."

"Is that what you think I'm doing?"

He smiled then, ruefully. "Only you know that, Lacey. But I do know one thing: you shouldn't settle for content. Go for happiness, wherever it is, however much it scares you."

"Says the man with no ties, the man who spends his life apart from everyone."

"I never said I was happy. I don't know how to be. But you could be. You should be."

"Happiness," she said, cradling her hot chocolate, "comes in many guises. Many of them in chocolate form. Don't worry about me, Zac. I'm fine. It's all under control." She stood up gracefully. "If I were you I'd spend more time worrying about my own happiness. At least I've managed content. Can you say that?" She took a couple of steps then paused, turned, and dropped a light kiss on his head.

Zac sat, the imprint of her lips burning its way right down to his toes, her words burning their way into his brain. He had money, success, the security he had always dreamed of, the security he had fought for. But did he have contentment? He wasn't even close. And for the first time in a really long time he was realizing what a huge hole that had left in his life. He had no idea how to fill it in or if he dared to try and work it out. He'd accused Lacey of being too scared to love but the truth was he was far, far more of a coward.

LACEY HAD ALWAYS been the kind of person to enjoy an uninterrupted night's sleep, one welcome bequest from her childhood. She'd spent so many years in hotel rooms, friends' houses, rental houses, sleeping backstage, on airplanes, in cars, that she generally just closed her eyes and she was out for a full eight hours.

Although she wouldn't exactly call herself a morning person once she had woken up Lacey was usually quick to get going. She loved her work so much that weekdays and weekends were all the same to her. But after a night tossing, turning, and fighting Patchwork for the blankets and quilts she woke up bleary-eyed and, for once, thoroughly Monday morningish. It took longer than usual to tame her hair and dress and by the time she stomped into the kitchen looking for coffee she was running late and had decided that the sooner Zac Malone finished his work and left Marietta for good the better.

Sure she sometimes wondered what it would be like to work somewhere bigger, what it would be like to only have to worry about her own show, not the advertisers, the schedule, vacation cover, and cleaning the washrooms. But that was normal, right? And sure, sometimes she wondered whether she could make something bigger than the few corporate videos she had shot for a few of Marietta's businesses to put on their websites. She wondered if she could make something that would make a difference. The kind of documentary that had attracted her to her media degree in the first place.

But no one could live their lives on *what if* and staring over at the lush green grass on the other side. She had a good job, lots of creative freedom, a wonderful home, and a place in the heart of the community she adored. And if the white picket fence was still a long way away well, she was only twenty-five. There was plenty of time to meet someone and settle down. All the time in the world.

"Morning," she said as cheerfully as she could, not wanting either of her great-aunts to notice or comment on her bad mood. She headed straight for the coffee pot only to skid to a halt as she noticed the long jeans-clad legs and lean torso leaning against the counter. "Why aren't you at work?"

"Morning to you too," Zac said cheerfully and Lacey clamped her mouth together to stop a snarl. How could he look so refreshed? Like he'd never had a bad night's sleep in his life. She eyed him resentfully as she sidled past and grabbed the coffee pot.

"You're usually at work at this time, that's what I meant." Her gaze dropped to his jeans. "And you're not usually so casual. It is Monday isn't it?" Maybe she'd dreamt everything. No failed pies, no almost kisses in the snow, no heart-to-hearts to leave her questioning everything that had seemed so simple before Zac arrived in Marietta. She reached out for a cup and a twinge in her side confirmed that yesterday had happened. She only had a couple of bruises, thankfully, but they were making themselves felt.

"I need to spend today on my firm. Some admin tasks, a few tenders to check, that kind of thing, so I'm working from home."

Home. Such an easy word and yet a word that meant so much. "Oh. Great." She didn't know what else to say, where to look, so she pulled her phone out of her pocket and began to scroll through her messages. As she did so a reminder popped up and she squinted at it. "Hoffmann tour. What does that mean?"

"Didn't you promise to go over to the Summer House and do a marketing video for the realtors?" Aunt Priscilla reminded her as she bustled out of the pantry, her mass of chestnut hair as yet unbrushed and a startling contrast to her bright red Cherry Ripe sweatshirt.

"Did I? Oh, darn it. I did. Was that this morning? I completely forgot. All this Bake-Off stuff put it right out of my head."

"You can't cancel, Lacey; Mrs. Hoffmann is counting on you. It's a big enough wrench for her to sell the house in the first place. We should try and make it as easy for her as possible."

"No, I'm not going to cancel." Lacey frowned as she pulled up her schedule and squinted at it. "I'm okay for this morning, I just need to make a couple of calls and let them know I won't be at the radio station until after lunch. The only thing is I meant to organize for one of the interns from the high school to come with me. It's easier with two when I need to rearrange the light or sort out backdrops. But I completely forgot and it's too late now. Never mind, I'll cope."

"How long is it going to take? Maybe I can help you," her aunt suggested.

"A couple of hours but I won't be able to go there until ten. Mrs. Hoffmann doesn't receive visitors before then. At least this gives me a chance to spend a couple of hours on my Bake-Off footage this morning."

"Not until ten? In that case it won't work. I'm sorry, dear, but your Aunt Patty and I are working on the Browns' wedding cake today and I can't get started that late."

"No worries, I appreciate the offer."

"Why don't I help?"

Lacey swiveled and fixed Zac with a glare. "I thought you had tenders to do."

"I do," he said mildly. "But my schedule's my own. I don't mind getting started now and working a little later if you need a hand."

What she needed was some time away from Zac Malone. Lacey opened her mouth, a polite refusal on her lips, when Aunt Priscilla forestalled her. "How wonderful. That's perfect, isn't it, darling? Thank you, Zac."

Lacey's mouth snapped shut.

"No worries," Zac said. "Call me when you're ready, Lacey. Thanks for breakfast, Mrs. Hathaway."

"Aunt Priscilla to you, young man."

He strode to the kitchen door before turning and fixing Aunt Priscilla with one of his most devastating smiles. "I could never be so irreverent. I'll see you all later. Whenever you're ready, Lacey."

She nodded. So much for keeping her distance from Zac. Unless... Lacey darted a suspicious glance at her great-aunt. Aunt Priscilla looked innocent enough as she flipped through a cookbook, humming to herself as she did so, but there was telltale tilt to her mouth and a self-satisfied set to the plump shoulders. "You do know he's going to leave in a few weeks."

"What, dear?"

That innocent voice wasn't fooling Lacey, not for one moment. "Zac—he's heading back to San Francisco as soon as this contract is done and there's no reason for him to come back to Marietta. Just don't get too attached." But Lacey didn't know if her warning was aimed at her great-aunt—or at herself. Either way she was pretty sure it was falling on deaf ears.

Chapter Twelve

SUMMER HOUSE WAS also on Bramble Lane, just a few houses along from Crooked Corner. It was a huge, imposing Victorian mansion—rounded, witches' hat-topped towers on both sides giving it the appearance of a medieval castle. Although Mrs. Hoffmann had a veritable army of gardeners, handymen, and maids to help her keep the house up it still felt like a place that had seen better days.

"Apparently Mrs. Hoffmann's father used to hold amazing garden parties," Lacey told Zac as they climbed the steps to the front door. "There are pictures in the Marietta archives of croquet matches on the lawn and children playing hide-and-seek. It's funny to think of all the people who have climbed these steps, long since dead and forgotten. When they were dancing the Charleston and drinking cocktails under the eyes of the prohibitionists they must have felt invincible, that life and youth would always be theirs, and now they're nothing but forgotten photos in albums no one looks at anymore."

He shot her an unreadable glance. "I've never thought

about the world that way."

"Really? I can't help but think about the past, especially here on Bramble Lane. When this house was built women still wore crinolines—imagine! It's seen two World Wars, flappers and flower children, horse-drawn carriages, and solar energy. Poor old thing." She patted the porch balustrade affectionately. "No wonder it's tired."

"It's always belonged to one family?"

Lacey nodded. "Mrs. Hoffmann's grandfather built it at the end of the nineteenth century, her father inherited it, and then when he died it was passed to Mrs. Hoffmann. But her only son died in Vietnam and so there's no one to inherit. It's sad. Who's going to buy a place like this?"

"It needs some work," Zac said standing back and assessing the shingles on the roof. "It will probably end up as another B&B or bought by a developer and turned into condos."

"Such an end of an era. I'd like to see garden parties on the lawns again. Croquet and iced lemonade and children running around. This is a house that needs a family."

"A large family—it must have at least ten bedrooms."

"Oh, at least," Lacey agreed as she pressed the bell. It tolled solemnly and they waited for a short while until the front door swung open.

A middle-aged woman peered out at them. "Yes?"

"Hi." Lacey held out her hand and smiled. "I'm Lacey Hathaway. I'm here to do the video, for the realtor?"

Her smile wasn't returned. "Come on in."

Lacey raised an eyebrow at Zac before accepting the grudging invitation. The double doors opened into a large octagonal room, a piano on one side and a magnificent sweeping staircase on the other. Two uncomfortable-looking formal chairs were positioned around a polished wrought-iron fireplace and a highly polished round table in the middle of the room held a staggeringly ugly vase filled with dried flowers. The woman held her hand out for their coats. "I expect you'll want to see Mrs. Hoffmann before you go traipsing through the house?

"Yes, please. If she's up to it."

"It's a shame that's what it is. Chasing an old lady out of her home," the woman grumbled as she ushered them into a sunny room directly off the hall. Books lined two walls, a fire danced in the grate, and three couches surrounded a low square coffee table. Lucia Hoffmann lay on one sofa, a delicate lace blanket over her knees. Like her house she was a relic from another era but despite her evident age and frailty her gray eyes were intelligent and keen.

"Hello, Lacey, very kind of you to help me with this."

"It's my pleasure, Mrs. Hoffmann. This is Zac Malone. He's going to give me a hand today, if that's okay."

"Absolutely. Carola, can you bring my guests some tea? Coffee?"

"Tea would be lovely," Lacey said and Zac agreed. Carola tossed her head and stomped back out to the hallway. Mrs.

Hoffmann sighed as she watched her go.

"Poor Carola. She thinks I'm being driven out of my home. But it's been too much for me for many, many years. I just wasn't ready to leave my ghosts behind." Lacey followed her gaze as it traveled over the photographs and portraits dotted on every surface and spare bit of wall until it rested on a large portrait of a handsome man in his late fifties. The man was smiling but there was a lurking sadness in his eyes that drew the viewer in.

"I'm sure your ghosts will travel with you," Zac said with such gentleness Lacey felt tears start in her eyes. She swallowed hurriedly. She would be no use to anyone if she allowed herself to get emotional about a house!

But this was more than a house. Four generations of Mrs. Hoffmann's family had loved, quarreled, eaten, played, made love under this roof and now they were all gone except for the pale, silver-haired old lady.

"What do you need from me, Lacey?" Mrs. Hoffmann asked after tea and little sugar cookies had been served. "Would you like me to tell you a little about the house and the family who lived here or would you rather just wander round alone and film whatever you need? I don't mind either way."

"The realtors know what a special house this is," Lacey said thoughtfully. "That's why they wanted me to produce a proper film for their website, not the usual quick walk-through filmed on someone's phone. If you did want to talk to me about your family, about the people who lived here, I could use it as a soundtrack to the tour and that would certainly add some character to the video, but only if you're up to it."

"I'm always up for reliving my memories. I hate to think that when I leave this house my family will be forgotten."

Lacey took her camera out of her bag and switched it on. "Your family will never be forgotten; they're at the very heart of Marietta. If it's okay with you, Mrs. Hoffmann, I'll ask you some questions and film while you answer. I'll show you the video when it's done and anything you don't like will be edited out; but whoever buys this house will be buying a piece of Marietta history and I think we should make that as clear as the size of the rooms and number of baths, don't you?"

"Let me sit up straight then. I don't want to be filmed lying down—most undignified." The older lady folded the blanket and laid it to one side, slowly moving her legs down off the couch, smoothing her skirt until she sat up straight-backed and proud, her hands clasped in her lap.

Lacey honed the camera in on her. "Your grandfather was one of the earliest settlers here wasn't he?"

Mrs. Hoffmann smiled. "He was. He was born in New York and, like many Americans, Ted Bartlett headed West looking for a chance to make his mark. Even though Marietta was nothing but a two-horse town when he got here, he saw which way the wind was going. The copper mining bubble was bursting by then and ranching beginning to draw people in. He figured that cattle needed feed and he invested the money he'd saved working on the railroads in a mill. When that did well he built a paper mill to take advantage of all the felling that was going on and he invested in transportation too. Within five years he was one of the richest men in town. Of course, rumor has it he had his fingers in many pies, legal or not. I couldn't possibly comment on that!"

"Did he marry a local girl?" Lacey panned the camera over to the series of black and white photographs on the grand sideboard, focusing on the very oldest, a suited, bearded man standing beside his seated wife, a fat baby, all curls and ribbons, perched on her knee.

"He did. My grandmother was a homesteader's daughter, as canny and hardworking as her husband and much more thrifty—my father told me, she always said a house the size of Summer House was too prideful for normal folk but my grandfather said a man's home was his castle and a castle was what they would have! I never knew her; she died of a broken heart they say after her two youngest sons went over to France in 1917. Neither of them ever came back."

Lacey slowly moved the camera over to the next photo: two smiling, boyish men in uniform, arms around each other's shoulders, looking more as if they were headed on a great adventure than as if they were heading off to war. "How terrible. Your poor father, losing both his brothers."

"He felt so guilty. He was exempted. He was running the

mills by then and they were temporarily turned over to war use. He always said he should have gone and kept an eye on his brothers. They were only eighteen and nineteen when they enlisted. Just boys. I guess that's why I feel so sad about getting so old, about being the last of the line, that there's no one who will remember Samuel and Joshua Bartlett. My father used to tell me bedtime stories about their childhood. They were wild boys, wild and spirited and good-hearted."

"When we're done here today," Lacey said, "let's make a date and I will come back and record everything you can remember of those stories. I'll send the recording to an oral library. They won't be forgotten, I promise." She felt Zac's gaze, intent on her as she spoke, an unspoken approval that warmed her through.

"I'd like that; thank you, dear."

"So your father inherited the house and the mills?"

"He did. My grandfather died not long after I was born and I was raised right here in Summer House. My father met my mother when he went back East for a short while. She was Boston born and used to society ways. She agreed to live in Marietta if she could raise the children the way she wanted and my father agreed; but unfortunately for them there was only one child and I was a real trial when I was young. Stubborn and wild, just like my uncles! My mother would hold garden parties and other entertainments and I'd usually have a rip in my skirt, grass stains on my stockings, and my hair would be wild. Oh, how she despaired. Especially when

I got older. She and my father wanted me to settle down and marry a nice young man of their choosing who would take over the mills."

"And did you?"

"What do you think?" Mrs. Hoffmann smiled and in her grin it was easy to see the wild young girl she had once been. "I insisted on college first and then just after I graduated the United States entered the Second World War. I had turned twenty-one and so I took my fancy degree from a fancy college and enlisted in the Women's Auxiliary Corps. Oh, my parents were mad. Looking back I realize they were just worried. I know how it feels, now, to have your only child sent overseas and not knowing if you'll ever see them again, but at twenty-one and with the prospect of traveling overseas I was too excited to care."

"But you came back to Marietta and to Summer House after the war ended?"

"Eventually." Her voice softened. "I met Karl in Berlin. I was a driver for a US general and he was our interpreter. He hadn't lived in Germany for ten years. He'd been sent to live with his English aunt after his brother was arrested for anti Nazi activity."

She stared into the distance. "Karl never did find out what happened to him although he never stopped looking, right until he died. It was shocking for him, seeing what had happened to his country, to his people. He was anti Nazi, not anti German. Still, when I came home engaged to a Karl

Hoffmann, a man who, despite ten years in England, still had a German accent, it was *not* well received. My father threatened to disinherit me, my mother took to her bed, and more than one neighbor refused to acknowledge me. Once someone threw a stone at me as I walked down the road."

"Here in Marietta?"

"Oh yes. People had lost sons—my own uncles had been killed in the last war so I understood the sentiment. But how could we recover from such devastation without love and forgiveness? I told my parents I could settle in London, or Germany, or New York or here in Marietta but wherever I settled it would be with Karl and if it was to be in Marietta they had to accept him. They agreed to meet him, traveling to New York when he arrived in the States. After the first night my father gave us his blessing—and Karl ran Bartlett Mills until we finally sold up twenty years ago."

"A happy ending."

"We were very happy, mostly. We lost our way a little in the early seventies after our son died. We named him Samuel Joshua after his great uncles. Ironic isn't it, that he also died fighting on foreign soil?"

Lacey panned to the final photo, another smiling young man in military uniform, hair short in a regulation cut. He looked so young. Too young. "I can't imagine how you felt."

"Those were dark days. There were times when I didn't think I could get up the next morning and yet somehow I did. And then the next and then the next. And then one day

I laughed at something and I realized I hadn't laughed in over a year. Karl and I struggled with Sam's death in different ways and it nearly drove us apart; but in the end love, our love for each other, our love for our son, was strong enough and we made it through. That's why, in spite of everything, despite being alone now, I feel blessed that I was lucky enough to have such love, that I had fought for it and didn't fritter it away. I often wondered what would have happened if Sam had come back to us. If he and Patty Hathaway might have made a match of it like they always planned."

"My great-aunt Patty?" Was this the tragedy that Patty kept locked away? It would explain why she had never married. She was a true Hathaway through and through. Once her heart was given there was no other path for her. Lacey laid the camera down and got to her feet, walking over to the sideboard to pick up the photo and study it: the blond hair and blue eyes, the smattering of freckles. "He has such kind eyes."

"He was the loveliest of boys. Such a sunny disposition. He and your Aunt Patty dated right through high school. They were prom king and queen, you know."

"Aunt Patty was prom queen? She kept that quiet!"

"When you come back I'll show you photographs. They were such a striking couple. I have letters too, all the letters she wrote Sam from all over: New York, London, Paris. Every week a letter arrived, pages thick—and in those days the cost of airmail letters was considerable. Even when Sam was away they arrived and I kept them for him when he came home. Only he never did. I meant to give them back to her when she came back to Marietta but somehow I couldn't. She's visited me, of course, but we never have talked about Sam, even after all these years. Maybe we should. And she should have her letters. I never read them of course but I liked having them, a reminder of what could have been." She smiled at Lacey. "So, we could have been related by marriage."

"I'd have liked that."

"I would as well." Mrs. Hoffmann reached out and Lacey took her hand. "Very much."

"I'd better get on with the rest of the house. May I come back? To get the oral histories and to see the photographs?"

"Any time you like. And, Lacey? Maybe you could ask your Aunt Patty to come on over. Tell her I need to return some letters to her."

IT WAS HARD for Zac to concentrate that afternoon. The visuals and emotions conjured up by Mrs. Hoffmann repeated over and over in his mind. Tragedy upon tragedy, sons lost too soon, families torn apart. And yet, at the end, even though she was alone, the last of her family, she still had the grace to appreciate what she had had, gave thanks for the good. How did she manage that?

He shifted in his seat. It had never occurred to him to look for the good in his past; the negative had been so all-encompassing, so overpowering. But there had been good parts too. His early childhood had been picture perfect. Should he discount that because it felt like it was based on a lie? But his parents had been happy once...

Several teachers had believed in him. His boss on the construction site had treated him like a son. Zac might have always turned down the invitations to Thanksgiving and Christmas dinners but they had still come with annual regularity. When was the last time Zac had emailed or called him? Far too long ago.

His college roommate had asked him to be his best man. He'd declined, reluctantly agreeing to groomsman duties instead, somehow still part of the wedding despite all his attempts to get out of it. What did Justin see in their friendship that made him so persistent despite Zac's stand offishness? What did he see in Zac?

"I fought for love," the old lady had said. "I didn't fritter it away." If Zac still had his health and wits at ninety would he be able to say the same? Would he have memories and ghosts to keep him company or would he be alone, having frittered away every chance of happiness?

Lacey had known just what to say, how to prompt the story without breaking the flow, how to encourage her speaker. It had made for a powerful narrative, one that had stayed with him as they had toured the graceful old mansion, Lacey's camera lingering on the stained glass in the old windows, on the perfectly carved balustrades, on each curve in the turret rooms. The house was still full of furniture that must have been bought when the house was newly built: chests and tallboys and whatnots, elegant beds and quilts faded with age. The whole house was an antique dealer's dream.

Glancing at his screen he realized it was time for dinner. Either he'd have to skip pie-making practice tonight or take some more time to catch up on his work tomorrow—which meant he'd be unlikely to wrap up his project and get out of Marietta as quickly as he'd hoped. He pushed his chair back and stood up then paused. Where was the sinking feeling? The annoyance? The frustration? He didn't feel any of it. In fact, if he had to put a word to the warm glow, then that word was pleased.

Dinner was already on the table when he arrived in the kitchen, a pot of chicken and dumplings served with the famed green beans and mashed potatoes. Lacey was in her place, camera set up in front of her, sifting through the still photos she had taken in addition to the video footage. "Look at the light in the attics," she said as he passed by. "Wouldn't it make a wonderful studio?"

"Is that Summer House?" Aunt Priscilla said, patting Zac on the shoulder as she passed by. Just a few days ago he'd have stiffened at the casual intimacy but he simply slid into his seat with a wink in her direction. Eating in the kitchen had become a habit but so had feeling like he belonged, only it had happened so slowly he had barely noticed the change.

But he didn't belong. He was a stranger passing through, wasn't he?

"Mmm," Lacey said. "I hate the thought of it not being a home anymore."

"But who could afford to live there?" her aunt pointed out.

Zac didn't consider himself sentimental but he could see why Lacey was nostalgic about the old house. "There's plenty of space if you wanted to turn some of it into an office. Maybe a doctor or a therapist or some internet start-up could move in? Offices on the first floor and live on the second?"

"Or a family where both mom and dad work from home and need separate office space. I'll try and subliminally send that message out in the video."

At that moment Aunt Patty appeared, entering the kitchen as if she were still on the Paris catwalk, grace in every line of her body. "Zac, I want to thank you."

Zac had just picked up the water jug and started to fill the glasses. He paused, the jug at a tilt. "Me?"

"Yes, you. I went to see the Evanses today."

Zac realized the water was still dripping from the jug and hurriedly filled the remaining glasses, setting the jug with care in the middle of the table. "Oh?"

Patty folded herself into her chair and nodded an agreement to her sister-in-law who began to heap the pot roast onto her plate. "That's enough, Priscilla, thanks. Yes, I found a pretext to call around and I am so glad I did. You know, Lacey, this is a real lesson in sharing responsibilities in a house. Harold and Celia Evans were so traditional—she did everything *in* the house and he did everything out. He can barely open a can, has no idea how to use a computer. She took care of all the finances, all the day-to-day managing, cooking, cleaning, shopping. He hasn't a clue, poor man, and Ty is little better though doing as much as he can, poor kid. Dementia," she said. "Poor Celia. Sudden and fast from what I can tell. Harold is having to care for her completely."

"Poor Ty, no wonder he's been looking so tired and unkempt." Lacey looked over at her aunt. "What can we do?" And there it was. Her automatic first response. How could she help? How could she make it better? Lacey might say she was a doer to give herself a purpose, to join in, but she was wrong. She cared about her community from the bottom of her heart.

"You know what they're like, so proud. Won't accept charity and didn't want anyone to know in case they thought they weren't coping and tried to put Celia in a home—or send Ty back to his mom. His grandparents have custody but it was contentious," Patty told Zac. "You know, this has been under our noses for the last six months and not one of us picked up on it till Zac mentioned his concerns for Ty. Thank you, Zac. I'll be meeting up with the Ladies' Aid tomorrow and we'll look at what help we can provide. Poor Harold, he's exhausted."

"Glad I could help in some way." They weren't just words. A glow spread through him, warmth at the knowledge that the intervention might be in time, that Ty might be saved from the evils of loneliness and despair.

Zac looked around the table at the three women, all talking rapidly as they discussed the best way to help the Evans family, his gaze honing in on Lacey. Her eyes were bright and she was waving her fork in emphasis as she drove her point home. He had stopped despairing when he'd left Connecticut and taken firm hold of his own destiny. But loneliness? He'd clung to that like a badge, resolving that nobody would ever get close enough to hurt him again. But maybe by his intransigence he'd just ended up hurting himself. Because now he'd had a taste of what it was like being part of a family, Zac didn't know how he was going to go back to his vagabond solitary existence.

Or how he was going to leave this newfound family behind.

Chapter Thirteen

MARIETTA SURE WAS a town that liked its festivals. There was nearly a week to go till Valentine's Day, a day Zac usually took about as much notice of as he did reality show gossip, but this year there was no avoiding it. Heart-shaped bunting had sprung up all through the town, including Crooked Corner, and the aunts were insisting he make his pie in a heart-shaped dish, which was adding to the complexity more than he was comfortable with.

The last two bakes had been of a high standard but neither had felt like winners. Another night, another practice. He was sick of the smell of ginger—still, at least he was enjoying a cupboard-love popularity at work with all the practice food he was bringing in.

He ducked to avoid a piece of bunting that had come unmoored and trailed damp hearts into the faces of any passersby. No, he didn't do Valentine's in any shape or form usually but this year he really ought to get the women of Crooked Corner a token of his appreciation for their welcome. Chocolates or something. But chocolates didn't seem adequate to express his feelings to Lacey. It would, he thought, be helpful if he knew what those feelings were.

He liked her. Respected her. Wanted her. But he knew that wasn't enough for her. Lacey wanted her white picket fence with no deviations from that path and he had no intention of trying to seduce her away from her dream. No, he either stayed her friend as he had offered, no flirting, no almost kisses, no meaningful moments or he...

That was the bit Zac was stuck with and no amount of evening walks seemed to give him an answer. Just because he had enjoyed the last few weeks, just because he had experienced a warm glow from helping Ty and his family, just because he was beginning to know his way around Marietta, just because the Java Cafe knew his coffee order and Sage his favorite chocolate, just because he was comfortable... None of that meant he belonged here. None of that meant he was going to up haul his life and start again.

None of that meant he was going to make himself vulnerable.

Besides, Lacey probably wouldn't want him to hint at anything long-term. He shouldn't mistake a bit of flirtation and her warm heart for genuine interest. Finding out if her feelings ran deeper was far too dangerous. What if they did and he let her down?

Or what if they didn't? What if he wasn't enough for her? He didn't want to see pity cloud those blue eyes. He couldn't be made vulnerable again.

"Zac? Is that you?" He turned at the call and saw Patty Hathaway walking briskly through the snow. Most people in Marietta wore some kind of thick padded jacket to keep out the cold but Patty was swathed in a thick, velvet-trimmed cloak that swirled around her like a royal robe. Her hat was more suited to a Russian spy in a sixties movie than a small town and her gloves fit so elegantly he suspected they had been made for her. Even though she was laden down with bags she still exuded a dignified elegance.

"Let me take those for you." Zac relieved her of the bulkiest bags and she fell into step alongside him as they headed away from Main Street and toward Bramble Lane.

"Thank you, dear. How was your day?"

"Good. All the accounts are up to date and audited and the software is installed and most of the migration of data is complete. By the end of next week I think it should all be ready to use and I just need to complete the training."

"And then you'll be leaving us."

"That's the plan."

A faint smile curved her lips. "Life is much more interesting when we don't plan, don't you think? It's the deviations and paths less traveled that are always the most rewarding I've found. Although—" her voice softened "—that could be because not all plans are destined to be."

Following her gaze Zac saw she was staring at Summer House, her heart in her eyes. "I don't know if Lacey mentioned…" He paused, diffidently. He had no idea how to approach anything as personal as a tragic love affair with the older woman—with anyone in fact.

"That Lucia Hoffmann has the letters I sent her son, safe after all these years? I have letters too. The letters that Sam sent me. I should probably let his mother read them. It would be the kind thing to do. I've clung on to them for all these years to remind me. Remind me it was real and not just some romantic dream."

"How did you know? That it was real? That this was the person you wanted to spend your life with, the person it was worth compromising yourself for?" He was afraid he'd given himself away with his impulsive question but Patty Hathaway was too lost in the past to notice.

"I didn't compromise anything. I thought I would have it all. Travel and adventures before settling down. He asked me to marry him, you know, straight out of high school. Ask me again in four years, I told him with all the arrogance of youth, all the certainty that we had all the time in the world. He was off to Yale and I wanted to see the world. I was certain he'd be waiting for me when I returned. The stupid thing was he needn't have gone."

"To Yale?"

"Vietnam. He was in college and an only son. That made him exempt twice over but he had a strong sense of duty. *See,* he wrote me, *you're not the only one who can travel. I'm going to see the world too.*" Her voice cracked and Zac's chest ached at the pain in her voice.

"I liked Mrs. Hoffmann. She seems like she was pretty independent herself back in the day."

"Oh, she was. I often wondered how much we'd have clashed if I had married Sam. Oh well, fate had other plans for me and I have had a full and varied life. I've lived in some wonderful places, experienced many wonderful things. I knew Sam wouldn't want me to stop living, that he'd want me to live enough for the two of us. The one thing I never thought I'd do was come back to Marietta if he wasn't here waiting for me, and yet here I am, living with my widowed sister-in-law and baking cakes for a living. I couldn't have planned that if I'd tried. But it's a good life. I just wonder..." She was speaking very quietly and Zac knew she had almost forgotten that he was there. "I wonder if there's an alternate reality where Sam and I live in that house and it's full of children and grandchildren and love and laughter. Lacey's right, for all its size it's a family house. I hope someday it is again."

Zac stared over at the stately old Victorian, at its turrets and porch. The house looked lonely, like it wanted to be filled with a family, with Christmas trees and heart-shaped bunting, with spring flowers and summer blooms and wreaths made of fall colors. It wanted boots and shoes tumbling around the porch and balls and bikes left on the drive. For all its size and grandeur it had been built to be a home, not a show house. "Me too," he said slowly. "Me too."

LACEY SET HER camera up in one corner so it took in as much of the kitchen as possible and her webcam on the counter she would be working on. She smoothed her hair before twisting it up into a loose knot. She tugged her pale blue sweater down and switched the webcam on.

"Good morning," she said with as sunny a smile as she could manage. "Today is Saturday and that means just one thing here in Marietta. Pie day! I'll be over at the Main Street Diner this afternoon to capture as much of the pastry action as I can to share with you later, but tune in in just half an hour to see me attempt this very same challenge and see if I can bake a pie that passes muster with the hardest judges of all: my aunts. I'll be honest with you, my practice sessions haven't gone as well as I had hoped. Pastry is hard, folks, but I'm staying positive and hoping today will be my lucky day. Don't forget this is all for a really good cause and the links to donate are on this very page. Thank you so much to everyone who donated after last week's cookie crumble disaster—you amazing people raised over six hundred dollars and every cent of that has gone straight to the fundraising appeal. See you soon."

She switched off the webcam and sank onto her stool, trying not to sigh. It had all seemed so simple just a few weeks ago. Nat would come home and try to bake and she, Lacey, would be at the heart of it all, publicizing, fundraising, and doing whatever she needed to do to make this whole Bachelor Bake-Off a success. And it was working. Her behind the scenes footage had been viewed hundreds of times, not just locally, and the Bake-Off had even been mentioned on the local state TV station when they were rounding up the forthcoming weekend's events. Jane was delighted and working hard to try and capitalize on the interest and get some of the press to come to the third and final Bachelor Bake-Off afternoon tea at the Graff Hotel a week today.

And then what? The Bake-Off would be over and Zac would head off and Lacey would be exactly where she had been when this all started. Where she had been since she was sixteen.

Maybe it was time to think about her future instead of assuming everything would just fall into place. Did she want to work at Radio KMCM forever or did she have dreams of something bigger, of expanding her horizons?

Or did she just want Zac's approval? She couldn't close her eyes without seeing him. Without seeing the crack in those granite cheekbones when he allowed himself to smile, without seeing the warmth and approval in his dark eyes she had begun to crave. Twice he had come to her, reached out. She knew he kept to himself, that his friendship was a rare gift. Was she greedy for craving more?

And what if he wanted the same things she did? What if he liked her beyond friendship and attraction? He hated small towns, she knew that. Disliked the attention and gossip and lack of privacy living in a small town entailed. All the things she loved about Marietta repulsed him. He wanted cities, constant summer, a job that took him from place to place, no real roots, no community. Lacey had lived that way for sixteen years. She never wanted to go back to that again.

If there was a middle ground she couldn't see it.

She looked up as the door opened, her heart speeding up painfully, thumping so loudly it competed with the grandfather clock in the hallway—only for disappointment to lurch its sickening way through her when, instead of Zac's lean figure, her aunt bustled in. *I have to stop behaving like a lovesick teenager*, Lacey told herself firmly.

"Morning, Aunt P."

"Morning, Lacey, all ready?" Aunt Priscilla opened up one of the big fridges and poked her head in, humming as she did so. "You and Zac won't mind if I'm in here while you do your mini bake-off do you? I've got the Carter christening cake to do and for insurance reasons I don't like to do commercial cooking in the house kitchen."

"Not at all—we could move if that helps?" Lacey offered but her aunt shook her head.

"Don't worry, dear, there's plenty of space for us all. You know, I have high hopes of Zac this afternoon. The pie works really well and he's got it down pat. It looks attractive too, which is so important. But then his cookies were much better in practice than he managed in competition. Do you think he suffers from nerves? That could make his hands warm and there is nothing more fatal for pastry."

"I don't think he's nervous. More of a perfectionist than anything. He's drawn up spreadsheets again you know. Every moment timed exactly. Cooking by numbers."

"Dear Zac," her aunt said unexpectedly. "What a wonderful addition to the family he is. He fixed the squeaking floorboard in my bathroom you know, and tightened the balustrade. I do like a man who's handy if you know what I mean."

"Yes," Lacey cautiously agreed pretending not to see the unsubtle wink. "But he's not one of the family you know, Aunt P. He's leaving soon and I don't think he has any reason to come back to Marietta."

"No reason at all?"

Lacey shook her head, hating the telltale heat stealing across her cheeks. "We're just friends if that's what you mean."

"You seem to be very good friends. I've seen the way you look at him, Lacey—and I've seen the way he looks at you. That's not friendship; at least we didn't call it that in my day."

"Aunt P, he doesn't want to live in one place, you know that. And I can't live on the move. What future would we have?"

"Do you have to decide that now?"

Lacey stared at her aunt in surprise. "What do you

mean?"

"You're young, Lacey. You don't need to fall in love with a mortgage and a savings account and a weekly chore list just yet. Why not have some fun before you worry about all that? Zac's a different man to the one who came here a few weeks ago. I don't think he finds Marietta so very dreadful now, do you?"

"Maybe not."

"He might not want to settle down here now, but that doesn't mean he'll never set foot here again. And it would do you good to spread your wings a bit. The station won't collapse if you take a vacation every now and then, go out of State at the weekend. It wouldn't be easy to date someone who doesn't live near you, admittedly, but it's not impossible. You youngsters with your smartphones and your FaceTime and video calling. Your Aunt Patty was prepared to spend a four-year courtship writing letters on paper no thicker than this." She brandished a tube of baking parchment at Lacey. "You could see Zac's face every day thanks to the internet. And other bits too, according to the news."

"Aunt Priscilla!" Lacey couldn't help laughing. "You are terrible. But I don't know if that's what Zac wants. We haven't even kissed. Twice I thought we might but once I put a stop to it and the second time he walked away as if nothing had happened. And he wants to fix me up with one of the other bachelors. If he wins today then he has two out of the three wins and that's my forfeit. Does that sound like a man thinking about a relationship to you?"

"It sounds like a man trying very hard not to think about a relationship. Lacey, honey, don't you think you should be having this conversation with Zac? What's the worst that could happen?"

"He could laugh."

"He won't laugh."

"He could say no," Lacey whispered, hating to admit her cowardice.

"At least you'll have an answer either way. I think you need some courage, Lacey."

"Or to win today so he can't set me up on a date."

"In that case," her aunt amended, "you need courage and a great deal of luck."

LUCK WAS NOT on Lacey's side. Despite blind-baking her pastry base it was undercooked and soggy, and the crumble she had so painstakingly rubbed together had clumped into unappetizing rock-like lumps. She grimaced at her webcam, hoping the viewing figures and subsequent donations would be worth this public humiliation. "I wish we kept pigs; at least this wouldn't be wasted. No human is going to eat this, that's for sure."

She swiveled the webcam to focus over on Zac. He looked completely unruffled, not a hair out of place, cool and crisp in a smart, short-sleeved, red shirt and his usual beautifully cut jeans. His workstation was neat and tidy in direct contrast to Lacey's, which looked as if she had let an entire day care center's worth of toddlers loose with a bag of flour. His pie sat smugly in the middle of the counter, the crust a honey gold and the crumble temptingly crisp and even.

"Just remember," Lacey reminded any web viewers. "Looks aren't everything. He could have used salt instead of sugar or over gingered the blackberries. I can still pull this off. Either way there's fifty dollars going straight to the appeal from whoever loses today—and I hope you'll all match it. Let's make my probable humiliation worth it."

Lacey didn't mind another fifty-dollar forfeit, especially as she knew it would prompt her online viewers to donate as well. It was the other forfeit she was less keen on. The one she wasn't going to share with the public.

Her date.

She'd met most of the bachelors now, interviewed five out of the eight for her show, and had chatted to all of them the week before. They all seemed like very nice, worthy men, but there hadn't been a single spark. Her pulse had remained even, her stomach calm, her heart untouched. But as soon as Zac came near everything changed. Her pulse speeded up to terrifying levels, her stomach swooped as if she were facing a black slope on inadequate skis, and her heart physically ached at the sound of his voice. She could keep her end of the bargain and go out on a date with the bachelor of his choice but she knew it would be no good.

The only date she wanted to go on was with Zac Malone.

"Are you ready for us to judge?" Her aunts had been working steadily over at the other end of the kitchen, weaving their usual alchemy and transforming their humble ingredients into a cake worthy of a christening. It was Valentine's themed and Aunt Patty had been shaping tiny rosebuds and hearts with her clever, deft fingers, to decorate the entire three-tier cake.

"Um…" Lacey looked down at her pie and winced. "I guess. I'm sure it tastes better than it looks." She'd added lots of sugar after all, and lots of maple syrup. Her blackberries had been sour at the weekend and never say she didn't learn from her mistakes. She'd upped the ginger as well, to try and stop her pastry being quite so bland. It might be soggy but at least it would have some zing to it. She hoped.

"Absolutely," Zac said with enthusiasm, returning Lacey's glare with a smile as he placed his annoyingly perfect pie next to hers. Her stomach rumbled. His did look and smell fantastic. She should try some, for fairness' sake.

The aunts stepped over, forks in hands, and surveyed the pies. Their smiles were proud as they looked at Zac's, muttering to each other about bake consistency and even spread. They were less proud and a lot more amused when it came to Lacey's. "It's supposed to be a crumble topping," Aunt Patty muttered. "Not a rock-filled landscape."

Lacey hadn't really held out any hope of winning but she conceded the second the pies were sliced. The slicer slid through Zac's with a satisfying crunch and the piece was extracted cleanly. The pastry was cooked through to the bottom, the berries firm, and the aunts both closed their eyes with a sigh of approval as they sampled it. Lacey's pie, on the other hand, made more of a squelching sound than a crunch and the piece disintegrated on extraction, a soggy mess oozing runny berries onto the plate. She held the plate up to the webcam. "There you have it. My best effort. That's got to be worth a donation or two? Aunt Patty, Aunt Patricia, would you like to announce the winner?"

"We do appreciate the effort you put in, Lacey," Aunt Priscilla said.

"Yes, yes. But?"

"But there are a few problems with your pie," Aunt Patty said diplomatically.

"What? Apart from the taste, the look, the consistency, and the fact that it's not baked?"

"It's also over sugared and over gingered and the pastry is both crumbly and undercooked."

"And your pie does have a soggy bottom," Aunt Priscilla chimed in. "Now Zac's pie is, I have to say, a delight. Crisp, the berries are the right side of tart, the ginger gives it a real zing and the syrup adds a darkly sweet tone. Really very well done, Zac."

Lacey fumbled in her pocket and pulled out her wallet,

extracting a crisp fifty and holding it up to the camera. "Strike two for me. If you can help out by matching my donation then please, every dollar counts. Tomorrow I'll be posting all the highlights from today's Bachelor Bake-Off including the judging, so please make sure you tune in and if you can get to Marietta for four p.m. then you can experience all the excitement for yourself. Through this week I'll be interviewing the last three bachelors and the Monroe family will be telling me what this fundraising means to them. I'll also be chatting to Chief Hale about the First Responders' plans when the house opens so if hunky silver fox fire chiefs are your thing, then Thursday is going to be your day. Thanks for watching."

She switched off the camera and turned, freezing when she realized Zac was right behind her, so close she could feel his breath on her face. "How do you do that?"

"How do I do what?"

He gestured at the camera. "Be so natural, so chatty."

"I don't know. I just say the first thing I think of."

"Isn't it intimidating, knowing all those people will be watching?"

"It's more intimidating to think they *won't* be watching and I'm broadcasting to fresh air. Besides, I don't post any personal stuff; it's all work. It all makes a difference and that's exciting." Lacey looked up at Zac. His eyes had softened, his smile heartbreakingly sweet. She searched his face for mockery or sarcasm but couldn't see any. Warmth flooded through her. "What? Why are you looking at me like that?"

"I won the challenge."

"I know." She waved the fifty-dollar note at him, trying to pretend she was cool and collected and that her pulse wasn't trying to outdo a runaway train. "Look, penalty right here."

"That's two out of three and that, Lacey Hathaway, makes me the overall winner."

How did the usually large kitchen feel so closed in and hot. Lacey glanced over at her aunts but, back at their own station and absorbed in their work, they seemed hazy, like they were in a different universe. All she could see or hear with any clarity was Zac.

"Double or nothing?" she offered, her voice croaky with nerves.

"Not this time. I'd hate to watch you crash and burn again."

"Okay. Your loss. Marietta really has a lot to offer the discerning traveler."

Zac wasn't to be dissuaded. "You owe me a date. With the bachelor of my choice."

"Yes," she agreed. "I do."

"Tonight."

"Tonight?" she almost squeaked. "But how do you know your chosen bachelor will be free? Or that he even wants to have a date with me? Will I be expected to take him out or are we going Dutch?" Had he been talking to the other bachelors about her behind her back? Did they all know about this bet and her sad loveless state? Lacey's stomach twisted.

"He is free, he very much wants to have a date with you, and no, you will not be going Dutch. Tonight is his treat. My treat."

"You are paying for me to go out with some random man?"

"Not a random man. With me. I'm the bachelor, Lacey. I chose me. What do you say?"

Chapter Fourteen

"**Y**OU WON!" LACEY twirled round in celebration. "You actually won. With a perfect score. Ryan Henderson said he would be proud to have made that pie. Proud! And Rachel shook your hand. I can't believe it. And did you see how much you made at auction? I swear, that pie took more than any real live bachelor ever could. Even George Clooney. Not that he's a bachelor anymore but when he was."

"You're saying my pie is better than George Clooney?" That was a compliment, right?

"You made the pie equivalent of George Clooney," Lacey confirmed. "The judges were practically swooning. You know what this means? Your cake is going to have to be off the charts incredible."

Zac shook his head. "Can we not talk about the cake now? Once this auction is over I am not going to as much as look at flour or butter for a year."

"No, that can't be. You have a talent, my friend, and such a talent can't be squandered. There's an ancient saying around here. A man who can make a perfect pie and fix a squeaky floorboard is worth his weight in gold."

"That's a strangely specific saying."

"Strange coincidence, huh?"

Zac grinned over at Lacey. She was particularly adorable dressed up for the cold wintry night, with her bobble hat and knitted gloves and thick jacket, her face glowing with the cold. "Very strange. Almost as if you made it up."

"Almost. Seriously, Zac, you were cool as a cucumber in there. Not a nerve to be seen. Very impressive."

"I was calm. I had already won you see."

"You had?" She wrinkled her nose. "You bribed the judges?"

"No. This morning. I won a date. This afternoon was just gravy."

"Oh." Her cheeks were even pinker as she took in his words. "Okay. Although to be honest, beating me was probably never in doubt."

"Not really," he admitted and laughed as Lacey swatted him indignantly.

"So, what are we doing on this date? Do I need to go home and change?"

"No, I don't think so. You're going to give me that tour of Marietta you've been promising me. Show me your town, Lacey, show me why it's so special. Whatever you want. I'll pay but you choose."

"Ice-skating and sleigh rides and hot chocolate in the snow?"

"If that's what you want, I'm in your hands."

She looked at him speculatively. "You may regret those words. Come on then, we have a town to explore."

It was no surprise that Lacey led him straight to the sleigh hire stop on Main Street. Zac usually rolled his eyes when he passed it, the sweetness of a sleigh stop jarring him every time. But tonight with the snow and the stars and an excited Lacey the idea didn't seem so overly quaint after all. It felt right.

Two brown horses were stamping and pawing at the snow and Zac eyed them uneasily. "They're docile as anything," the driver said cheerfully. Zac admittedly knew very little about horses but the last word he would have used to describe either animal was docile. Lacey had no such qualms, heading straight to their heads to blow warm air onto their noses, feed them mints, and whisper love words into their ears.

"Where to?" the driver asked.

"Just to Miracle Lake. Will that be okay?"

"Sure. Business is brisk tonight, it being the weekend before Valentine's Day." He winked knowingly at Zac. "I'm expecting several proposals in the back of that sleigh this weekend."

"How lovely." Lacey climbed into the old-fashioned carriage, the padded bench seat comfortably accommodating two. "Does it ever get old, listening to proposals? Or is each one perfect?"

"There's nothing nicer than sharing that moment," the driver confirmed, shaking out the folded blankets and handing them to Zac. Zac climbed in beside Lacey and adjusted the blankets over them. It was curiously intimate being together under the same throws, for all they were in the open air and in public.

"Do any stay with you?" Lacey asked, pulling the faux fur rug a little tighter.

"The best are the impromptu ones. I've heard poems and carefully prepared speeches and seen men put on special music, and present their girlfriend with flowers and chocolates. This summer there were at least two flash mobs, which I really prefer not to have to deal with because they spook the horses. But the ones that seem the most romantic to me are the ones where he simply says he can't imagine spending the rest of his life without her. They usually bring a tear to my eye." He swung himself into his seat and clicked to his horses who tossed back their heads, the sleigh bells ringing as they did so.

"Look, Zac, the bells are in the shape of hearts."

"Is there anything in Marietta that doesn't get covered in hearts over Valentine's Day?"

Lacey shook her head. "No. We like our holidays."

"I've noticed. So what about you, Lacey? Would you say you're a flash mob kind of girl or would you prefer poetry?"

She wrinkled her nose as she thought. "I'm comfortable in front of a camera or a crowd, you know that. But to me a proposal is something private, intimate. I know these big, public proposals are a lot of work and effort and that's really sweet but I would rather something small and from the heart. To be on a walk or just hanging out and it being kind of spontaneous and right rather than planned. How about you?"

"I think it's highly unlikely I'll ever be part of a flash mob," Zac admitted and Lacey's peal of laughter outdid the sleigh bells.

"I can't see that either. A spreadsheet of pros and cons though."

"Absolutely. And a fully costed breakdown."

"Nothing says romance like a breakdown of costs."

The sleigh took the same route through the woods he and Lacey had walked just over a week ago. The walk when they had agreed to be friends. She stilled as they passed the spot where he had almost kissed her and he knew she was remembering that walk too.

"Regretting our bargain?"

"Maybe a little," she admitted honestly.

Zac slid his gloves off and reached out to take her hand, removing her glove as he did so. It was a curiously intimate gesture, pulling at each fingertip before slipping the glove off. He swallowed, his heart thumping as her hand was bared and he entwined her fingers in his. No wonder the Victorians had set such store by gloved hands. "Me too."

"What do we do about it?" She stared down at their entwined hands.

"Do? We're on a date, aren't we? I'm no expert but that seems like the right place to start to me."

Lacey peeped up at him, her eyes huge in the starlight. "Yes, you're probably right."

They didn't speak for the rest of the ride, nor did they separate their hands. Zac sat back in his seat aware of little more than the feel of her soft hand in his, of the pressure of her fingers, of the way every nerve in his body seemed to be pulling him toward her. Her lips were slightly parted, and all he wanted to do was lean in and capture that lush mouth under his. But whatever this was, it wasn't a fast seduction. It was a courtship, a wooing. And it was a two-way thing. He needed to let her show him her town. He needed to know if there was space for him in her life and if so if he would be comfortable fitting in there.

But either way, at some point tonight, he vowed, he would kiss her. Even if it was just once he had to know what it would feel like, how she would taste. He'd allow himself that at least.

"YOU ARE A skate shark," Lacey said indignantly. "A skate shark and a ski shark. What other hidden talents have you kept from me?"

Zac skated a loose, relaxed curve, testing each blade as he

did so before fetching up alongside Lacey with a stylish turn that made her blink in envy.

"I played hockey up to junior high," he admitted. "And one of my jobs was at the local rink so I got plenty of ice time even when I couldn't afford to play."

She put her hands on her hips. "So when I was confiding my icecapade dreams to you, you could skate like this all along and didn't think to mention it?"

He put his hands up, laughing. "Hey, I just like to skate. I've never dreamed about spangles and medals. I don't need music and emotive choreography. Besides, you said you wanted someone to go skating with and here I am. Much more fun than trying to hold up a nervous newbie, isn't it?"

Lacey couldn't stop the responsive smile curving her mouth. Zac was right. She'd fully expected to have a slow, painful session, towing a reluctant Zac behind her. Not that she hadn't expected him to pick it up quickly, as a surfer and snowboarder he understood balance, but it would have been frustratingly slow on her only ice time this season. Instead he'd strapped his skates on, stepped confidently onto the ice, and had soared off in a fast, graceful arc while Lacey was still fastening her boots. "You're right. It's just I would like to be better than you at one thing."

"You are." He took the hand she held out as she stepped onto the ice and waited for her to get her balance.

"Yeah? Because you beat me at skiing and baking and you are an amazing skater…"

"I can't sing or play an instrument. I couldn't talk a stranger into committing to a three-week public baking competition. I couldn't cajole a bunch of people online into donating to a cause far from their homes. I couldn't switch on a microphone and make every listener feel like a valued friend…" He paused and she tugged his hand.

"Go on."

"I think I'll save some for later. Wouldn't want you to get vain."

Lacey's heart stopped for a second. What did he mean by that? She didn't have time to think because Zac began to skate, pulling her along at a great speed, away from the tumbling kids and the cautious learners, out to where the ice was clean and there was plenty of glorious space. All she knew was the exhilaration of the cold night air as they sped along, the clasp of Zac's hand in hers and the sheer joy of speed.

Zac slowed as they reached the center of the safe skating area, twirling Lacey around as he did so. It was almost deserted, as if they were alone under the velvet black sky punctuated by a kaleidoscope of stars. "You know how to ice dance after all," Lacey said breathlessly as she came to a stop.

"No lifts," he warned her and she looked down at her jeans and bulky jacket and smiled.

"I'm not dressed for it anyway."

"You'd be cold out here in your lycra and spangles."

"True. But it would be worth it." She skated backward,

enjoying the way her body fell into the fluid movement and opening her arms as she turned. "I love how free skating makes me feel. You know?"

"Yes. I know."

He'd caught up with her and she touched his arm with one gloved hand. "Tag," she said and then skated away with as much of a burst of speed as she could manage, leaving him standing confused for a second before his eyes lit up and he was after her at an impossible pace. Laughing, Lacey wove around the ice, trying to escape Zac, but he was inexorable, anticipating her every move before she even knew she was making it.

Her head start gave her barely any leeway. Closer and closer to the edge of the lake she skated with no obvious way past him... Breathing fast she feinted to the left before dodging right and sprinting as fast as her skates could carry her but Zac had read her move and he was on her, pulling her close, dictating their direction as he towed her right to the edge of the lake where the trees shadowed the water.

"Got you."

"I guess so." Lacey looked up, laughter trembling, only for all desire to laugh to melt away as she saw the heat and determination in his face. She swallowed nervously, all too aware that his hand was in hers, his arm around her waist, and they were standing so close that barely an inch separated them. "You have."

"Have I?"

"If that's what you want."

Desire blazed in his eyes and Lacey didn't know whether to back away—or whether to step forward. All she knew was that she would fall without him to hold her. "If that's what I want," he repeated softly and she shivered. "I used to know what I wanted, Lacey, but it seems like nothing's clear anymore."

"Me too."

"And here we are."

"Looks like it."

His hand slipped from hers leaving her achingly cold for one brief moment, only to burn as he ran a gloved finger down her cheek. "I like you, Lacey Hathaway."

"I'm very likeable."

He gave her a ghost of a smile and her knees weakened at the sweetness in it. "I don't want to hurt you. I promised you I'd stay away." His eyes searched her face looking for answers.

"You did and you have. But I think I was wrong. I was playing safe as usual. Maybe it's time I took some risks."

He tilted her chin and stared into her eyes for one long moment, the blood roaring in Lacey's ears as she looked boldly back, every fiber in her screaming at him to just kiss her already. He groaned, as if the sound were torn from him and then, in one abrupt move, pulled her closer so that chest was against chest, leg against leg, and the arm round her waist was the only thing anchoring her to the ice, to the world. And as his head slowly bent toward hers and his mouth finally, finally touched hers, Lacey knew that she had finally come home and it was everything she had always wanted it to be.

"SO WHAT NOW?"

Lacey stole a nervous glance at Zac. How could he sound so normal? How could he stride along as if everything were the same as it had been before, as if they hadn't spent five minutes locked in each other's arms lost to the world. If that group of kids hadn't skated noisily by they might be there still. She ran her tongue over her lips, rejoicing at the slight swell in them, shivering at the sensory memory of his kiss.

Whatever happened she would never regret those five minutes. Never had she felt so alive, so desirable. And yet it had been the chastest of kisses, separated by layers of thermal and wool, in public, balancing on skates. The chastest and the most mind-blowing kiss imaginable.

"Food?" she ventured. After all, this was a date. "Dinner and a movie?"

"I like it, old school."

"I am an old-fashioned girl," she told him.

"That you are." It sounded very much like a compliment.

"Where would you like to eat?"

"Not the diner," Zac said wryly. "I'm going to get pastry-making flashbacks every time I set foot in there. Where else do people eat in this town?"

"There's Graff's but—" she looked down at their denim-clad legs "—we're not really dressed for somewhere so fancy." Plus Graff's was a formal date kind of place. A dress up and go out for dinner, hushed conversation and expectation kind of place. It was lovely but not what Lacey wanted for this night of discovery. She wanted something as sweet and as simple as skating on a lake. Something that didn't scream commitment.

"Rocco's! You do like Italian, don't you?"

"Love it. What's Rocco's?"

"It's the embodiment of every Italian restaurant cliché but the food is wonderful, the welcome genuine, and there's something really charming about it."

"It sounds perfect."

It was. Big plates of pasta, a small glass of red wine for Lacey and water for Zac, a warm welcome and a little table in the corner—not too obviously romantic but tucked away enough for Lacey to feel that Zac and she were the only people in the world. Almost groaning with gluttony they then padded slowly through the lamp-lit streets till they reached the cinema where Lacey refused popcorn for the first time in her life and sank into the wide, comfortable seats feeling like a boa constrictor who had swallowed a goat and needed at least a week to digest it.

Friday night was classics night in the smallest screen and to Lacey's delight Zac had needed little persuading to agree to Cary Grant and Deborah Carr rather than the shoot them up alien invasion blockbuster in the main screen.

"Is this a chick's film?" he asked as he folded himself next to her and she shook her head indignantly.

"It's a romantic classic."

"Chick's film," he confirmed with a nod. He peered past her and his eyebrows rose. "Why has that woman over there got a whole box of tissues?"

"It's emotional. It's about two people who love each other and misunderstandings and destiny and sacrifice and oh! You are just going to have to see for yourself."

"At least the seats are comfortable in case I need to sleep," he said and she glared at him.

"I'll poke you awake if you as much as close one eye."

There was no need for her to keep an eye on him. As soon as the lights went down Zac took her hand as if they were teens on a first date, his hand cool and possessive, his thumb tracing circles over her palm that had her dizzy with desire. It took Lacey a while to settle into the film, distracted by Zac's touch, his knee warm against hers, the strength in the thigh alongside hers, the scent of pastry and ginger and warm food and something else uniquely Zac enveloping her, making it hard to concentrate.

But slowly she settled down, enjoying the intimacy of his touch and able to follow the plot as Deborah Carr and Cary

Grant swapped witticisms and tried—and failed—to deny their growing attraction.

She laughed at one moment and felt the vibration of Zac's mirrored amusement and had that sense of rightness when two people find themselves in complete harmony. And then she was swept away, into a world of dressing for dinner and disapproving gossip, of gorgeous islands and a timeless New York where the protagonists tried to become the person they felt they needed to be to deserve a happy ever after.

"That was wonderful," she choked out as the credits finally rolled and catapulted her back to present-day Marietta. Zac passed her another tissue and Lacey took it gratefully, mopping up the last stray tears. "Did you enjoy it?" She peered up at him, looking for any trace of emotion.

"I did. But, do you think…" He paused.

"Think what?"

"That they would work out in the end? Do you think people can change for love? Or do they go back to being who they really are? The first argument about money and Cary Grant finds himself smoothly seducing another heiress and Deborah Carr decides picturesque poverty isn't all it's cracked up to be and bags her millionaire after all."

"I don't know." Lacey wasn't sure if this was a critique of the film or something else, something fundamentally more meaningful. "I guess it depends on the love, doesn't it? I mean, it can make some people selfish, jealous, and controlling, but I think real love means wanting what's best for the other person regardless of the cost to you, don't you? Of wanting to be a better person, a braver person because of them. I like to think they made it work and they loved each other more because they had to work at it and compromise, because it wasn't easy." She paused, embarrassed she'd said too much.

"I like your interpretation better." Zac got to his feet and held out his hand. "Come on, let me walk you home."

"Very convenient that it's on your way," Lacey teased him.

"Isn't it?"

"Zac?" She paused, searching for the right words. "I have had a really lovely time, thank you."

"No, thank you. You picked the itinerary."

She took his hand, marveling at how natural that gesture had become. Part of her wanted to suggest they did this again some time really soon, another to beg him not to come near her again because she was liking his company far too much. But, she didn't want to spoil this perfect evening with emotions, or worries about the future. If this was all they had then she needed to savor every second. So she said nothing as they fell into step together, as if they had been walking side by side their whole lives long.

Chapter Fifteen

"EVENING!" LACEY HALF danced into the kitchen, scooping Patchwork up off the kitchen chair nearest the stove and pressing a kiss onto his furry head as she did so. "What's for supper? I am starving. It's been good though. I got loads of footage of the Monroes, talking about Harry and touring the house. It's going to be really powerful."

She'd had half a mind to cancel, not sure if Zac would want to spend the Sunday with her after such an amazing Saturday evening but she'd had a stern word with herself. She had made promises and she had to keep them. Zac would understand. She was looking forward to seeing him tonight though…

"Meatloaf is in the oven keeping warm," Aunt Patty called from the pantry. She came out, wiping her hand on a tea towel. "Your Aunt Priscilla is out keeping Celia Evans company so that Harold can go to Grey's and have a drink with his buddies for the first time in far too many months and young Ty can relax and not feel responsible for the whole world. I'm modeling for the advanced art class, this evening. In a toga I believe, which is not exactly correct. I don't think women wore togas but apparently the drapes are challenging to draw. And of course they don't do life drawing on a Sunday, especially as we use the church hall. You'll be okay on your own won't you, dear?"

"Sure." Lacey's breath hitched. No aunts. That meant she and Zac would be alone. She loved her aunts dearly but for the first time she was seeing the downside of living with two elderly chaperones—chaperones who could read her like an open book with very large print. "I'll just serve up for me and Zac then…"

"Zac?" Her aunt turned and Lacey's stomach dropped at the mingled pity and curiosity on her aunt's face. "He's not here, Lacey. He got a call this morning and has had to head back to San Francisco for a few days. I thought he would have told you."

Lacey would have thought that too. She stared at her aunt. "Gone? But what about the Bake-Off?" She managed to swallow back the next plaintive cry: what about me?

"He'll be back Wednesday or Thursday. I know that means he barely has time to practice but it can't be helped. He has a job and a life elsewhere; it was good of him to spare us the time." Was that a warning in her aunt's voice? Don't get too close. He doesn't belong here with us.

She shouldn't have needed that warning. Right up till last night she'd been telling herself the same thing but then he'd taken her on that date and everything had changed. At least she thought it had. But he hadn't texted her or called or left her any kind of message. He'd just left. As if he were nothing but her aunt's lodger.

"What about his work here? Doesn't he have commitments? A contract?"

"He's ahead of schedule even with all the time he's put into baking. It sounded like a genuine emergency, Lacey." Aunt Patty sounded sympathetic and Lacey bit her lip. She didn't want to be the target of anybody's sympathy, not even a beloved aunt's.

"Oh, well," she said as airily as she could, dropping another kiss on Patchwork's compliant head before placing him back on her chair and crossing over to the oven. "The house will seem quiet without him here, which is odd seeing as he barely uttered one word that whole first week."

"He still doesn't say that much. Doesn't get much of a chance between the three of us," her aunt agreed. "Lacey, I'm not prying, dear, but I did think… It did seem… You and Zac have been very friendly. He's a lovely man but he has a life and business elsewhere and you, dear… Well, you're not very worldly. I'd hate to see you get hurt."

"We're just friends." Lacey's hand tingled in the spot Zac had caressed as she spoke the casual words and she touched it absent-mindedly. "I like him, he's nice, and I guess he's good-looking if you like tall, dark brooding types." It turned out she did but she didn't feel the need to confess that to her aunt. "But I know he's not from here and he's not planning on staying…"

"You can't tie a wanderer down," her aunt said softly. "I should know. I was one. They might choose to settle eventually but only when they're good and ready."

"I'm not asking him to stay," Lacey protested. But the truth was she was secretly hoping that he might just choose to do that very same thing. That if Marietta made him welcome enough he might decide it was time to stop running and…and what? Settle down with her and paint that picket fence?

Lacey stilled. He had never made any intimation that he wanted that kind of life. She'd been priding herself on being oh so sensible and yet all along she'd been building romantic castles in the air. "We're just hanging out, that's all. And if it should go any further, well, Aunt Patty pointed out two people can live on the opposite sides of the country and date nowadays—after all, you wrote Sam every week and you were right across the ocean."

"It wasn't easy though, Lacey. And I loved Sam. Very much. We'd been together for several years and I was certain he was where my future lay, but there were still temptations and doubts on both sides. By all means see where your friendship takes you, but be careful, darling. That heart of yours is too big."

And with that her aunt was gone, leaving Lacey alone with the cat, a plate of meatloaf, and her thoughts. What if Zac had no intention of trying to extend their friendship past the end of his stay in Marietta? And even if he did he hadn't made any attempt to let her know he would be out of town. That didn't bode well for any future communication.

Lacey pushed her barely touched plate away, even though she usually had at least two helpings of her aunt's spicy meatloaf. Was this turmoil in her mind just because Zac hadn't left her a message or was it more? Was it because through Zac she had taken a long, hard look at her life and was beginning to acknowledge that it wasn't as perfect and that she wasn't as happy as she had told herself she was?

She had loved every minute of the nine years she had spent in Marietta. Even when she had been at college she had considered Marietta home, spending far more time at her aunts' house than she had on campus. Turning the radio station from a small, purely volunteer-led amateur concern to a profit-making, professional station right at the heart of the community it served whilst holding on to the volunteer ethos still filled her with a glow of satisfaction.

Plus over the last couple of years she had been asked to do more and more videos for the community, both personal and for businesses. The Bachelor Bake-Off had added a new fundraising string to her bow; Lacey knew that viewers had pledged at least two thousand dollars and the Monroe footage hadn't even gone up yet. She was quietly confident that she could bring the total up to three thousand by the end of the week. More than worth all those extra hours spent filming and editing. Almost worth her own public humiliation in the mini bake-off.

So, yes, she had achieved a lot in the three years since she had graduated from college. Achieved it from the safety of her turret room like a fairy tale princess, but she shouldn't let that take away from her achievements—after all, if Rory Gilmore could return to Stars Hollow then there was no reason why Lacey Hathaway should feel pressured to move out and move on.

But the nagging question remained: what next? Where did she go from here and could that place be found in Marietta? Or was she settling before she had had a chance to live? There would always be a home here—she knew that— her turret room right here at Crooked Corner, or her bedroom back at Three Pines. Zac was right, darn him, she had all the stability in the world. She could venture forth in all confidence with her family at her back. After all, taking the next step didn't mean she couldn't come back. Or, if she was willing to travel and freelance then she could be based here and move where the work was, rather like Zac.

Like her parents. Everything she hadn't wanted from her life. But unless Marietta suddenly became a media hub she didn't have much choice. Stay still and stagnate or move on despite her reluctance and grow.

"What do you think, Patchwork?" she asked but Patchwork was busy giving one creamy paw a good bath and didn't respond. "You'd miss me wouldn't you?" One twitch of the ear was all she got but that was enough to encourage her. "Don't worry. If I do start to work away more I'll be back so often you won't have a chance to miss me. Marietta's my home and no amount of spreading wings will change that. But I promise you one thing, Patchwork. I can't and won't let Zac Malone be a factor in my decision no matter how perfect the date. After all, it was only one date. Not a relationship. Not a promise."

But her words rang hollow even to herself.

ZAC STRODE ACROSS his living room and looked out of the dramatic floor to ceiling windows at the spectacular view of San Francisco's skyline. When he'd decided to settle in the city he'd eschewed looking for a place to live in the iconic "painted ladies", not wanting anything quaint or historic, nothing to remind him of his hometown. The beauty of his penthouse condo had been its newness; nobody else had ever lived there. And, he conceded wryly, it showed.

The floor, kitchen units, and wall color were still those picked out by the building company and the furniture—sleek, modern, and fashionable—had been ordered by Katie, his PA. All he'd cared about was that it was state of the art, top quality, and straight from the manufacturers—only the very newest for the boy who had spent his teens in thrift shop garb.

But there was nothing in the apartment to indicate that

anyone had made a home there. No photos, no paintings, not as much as a vase or a single ornamental knick-knack. Not even a book; he read everything on an e-reader. He could walk away tomorrow and there would be no sign he had ever lived here.

The sparseness had been a choice. Things meant nothing to him after all. Home was a dangerous concept. The apartment was within an easy commute of Silicon Valley where his offices were based. He leased a suite of rooms in a building on the city side of the valley and if he had to deal with start-up employees skateboarding through the foyer or risk losing his own staff to the big tech utopias with their bagel carts and on-site dog crèches that was a small price to pay.

The work address gave his company clout and, much as he didn't want to admit it, he liked how it was a sign of success. Zac Malone was no longer the unfortunate kid working three jobs and hauling his deadbeat mom out of bars; he was the CEO of a Silicon Valley company.

Not that he spent much time actually in the Valley. The office was home to the admin staff, the twenty-four-hour support staff, and the technical whizzes who turned his software dreams into reality; but the trainers, auditors, and consultants were all home based and Zac had continued to spend most of his own time in the field.

But maybe that needed to change. He'd been fooling himself when he thought he could keep growing his business whilst never putting down roots. Employees and clients needed stability and a CEO couldn't delegate all his responsibilities. A man needed to grow up and acknowledge there was a point when the past stopped defining him. Had he reached that point?

He picked up his phone and scrolled through his contacts. There was nothing filed under L. He and Lacey hadn't exchanged numbers; they hadn't needed to. She'd always been there when he looked for her. Funny to think how annoying he'd found it at first. Now he was like a scent dog, sniffing in vain for that vanilla and cinnamon scent of hers, the apartment deathly quiet without the backdrop of babble, laughter, and chat.

Home had always been a dangerous concept. A word associated with betrayal and drama and loneliness. Not a place he was ever going to click his heels to get back to. He had been more than content to take his chances in Oz. But now it made him think of Crooked Corner, of cushions and cats and something always baking away in the oven. It made him think of Three Pines and three generations living harmoniously under one roof. It made him think of Mrs. Hoffmann surrounded by her photos, memories, and ghosts. Now it was somewhere he yearned for. Something he knew he was missing.

But home wasn't just a place no matter what the old adage claimed. Home was a feeling, a sense of completeness. Home was other people. People who loved and accepted you no matter what. Something Zac hadn't had for more years than he cared to count. Something he had been far too scared to look for, to allow in. The first sign of intimacy and he had walked away without a single backward glance. But he didn't think he could walk away again. Not this time.

His hands curled into fists. There were no guarantees. He'd spent his entire young adult and adult life making sure he wasn't vulnerable. Stepping toward another human being, asking them to let him in, to take a chance on him, would change that irrevocably. If he was rejected would he be able to rebuild those protective walls or once they were ripped down were they gone forever, leaving him exposed?

But he couldn't carry on the way things were. Not when he had the tantalizing glimpse of another way, another life. A glimpse of happiness. And if it didn't work then he would just have to pray that somehow he'd have the strength to get up, start again, and keep the faith that he was deserving of more than a sterile apartment, anonymous motel rooms, and night after night sitting alone working.

He turned toward his laptop. On, as always, spreadsheets set up as always. Although the work that had brought him rushing back had only taken a day to sort out it had been the kind of oversight that drove home to him that he needed to spend the bulk of his time on managing his company. That his name and reputation were on the line if anyone or anything screwed up. He should have left Lacey a note though, or a word. He just didn't know what to say to her.

How to tell her that Saturday night had been the most perfect night he had ever spent. That she had been the perfect companion. That he was coming back. Back to her if she would have him.

He stared at the laptop screen. At the lines and lines of data. At work that could—which usually would—keep him absorbed until long after midnight and then again all the next day. It would always be there. But would his other opportunities? Or was he in danger of losing them forever?

The emergency might be almost over but now he was back in San Francisco he realized there was a long list of things he had to do, things he should have taken care of long before. He wouldn't feasibly get back to Marietta before Saturday lunchtime and the final Bake-Off, and that meant he needed to practice here, actually use his gleaming, un-touched state-of-the art kitchen. He might need a few things first. Like actual ingredients. Cake tins. Weighing scales.

What ingredients? He pulled out a pad and pen and tapped the pen on the kitchen counter. A simple cake, something easy to execute. He didn't actually care about winning the Bachelor Bake-Off; he just didn't want to humiliate himself. So simple. No layers. No elaborate frosting. No fancy decoration.

Cinnamon to remind him of Lacey. Apples because she was sweet and wholesome with a refreshing tartness. Brown sugar rather than white to add some snap. Surely he knew enough about baking after the last two weeks to turn those ingredients into something that would pass muster? Getting the cakes right wasn't the thing that would be tricky. It was getting the girl that worried him. The stakes were high and Zac was ready to play.

Chapter Sixteen

WHERE ON EARTH was Zac? Lacey tried not to look at her watch yet again but her eyes were drawn back to the miniature clock face against her will. An entire three minutes had passed since she'd last checked. She had to get to Graff's to start prepping for her live broadcast and Zac still wasn't back from San Francisco—and as he was their bachelor she was obviously concerned. That was the only reason she was repeatedly checking her watch.

The only reason. After all he'd been gone nearly a week and she hadn't heard from him once. Not a "hi" or a "how are you doing?" No "I miss you." So that was that. Thank goodness she'd made the sensible decision not to factor Zac into any of her future plans. When she did finally lay eyes on him she would be dignified and remote and certainly not tell him how much she'd missed him. Even though she couldn't deny to herself that she really, really had.

"What if he doesn't come?" she asked finally and Aunt Patty looked up from the kitchen table where she was putting the final touches to a cake she'd made for the Evans family. The community might not be able to cure Mrs. Evans' dementia but they could and did make sure she and her family were fed, warm, and that her husband and grandson had time enough away from caring duties to cope with their situation.

She had bumped into Ty the evening before and he had muttered that the freezer was so full of casseroles and pasta bakes there was no room for any more. But behind the couldn't care less eye roll Lacey had seen a devout relief and gratitude. She thanked Zac from the bottom of her heart for calling their attention to the situation before it got worse.

Well, she would thank Zac if she was on any kind of friendly speaking terms with him, which she was not.

"Zac?" her aunt asked in some surprise. "He's meeting us there. Didn't I tell you?"

"No." Lacey tried not to grit her teeth. "You must have forgot to."

"His plane doesn't get in till midday so he said not to wait. He emailed me through a shopping list yesterday. Your aunt and I were planning a dark chocolate gateau with chocolate snowflake décor but he's asked us for apples. And cinnamon. I'm not sure that's going to wow the judges."

Lacey's mouth watered. She loved apple cake. "I suppose it depends on how he does it—and how the other bachelors do. Okay, in that case I'll head over now. Do you want a lift?"

Aunt Patty shook her head and Lacey raised one hand to

the messy bun she'd spent half an hour trying to make look chicly messy as opposed to incompetently messy. If she went for the same kind of achingly hip asymmetric bob as her aunt she would just look like she'd let a toddler loose on her hair. It was most unfair. "I'm picking up our table guests on the way. Your Aunt Patty and I have bought a whole table at the afternoon tea, as sponsors we thought we should."

"I know. I hope there's a seat for me. I love afternoon tea, so civilized."

Lacey checked she had her camera, microphone, and battery pack before setting off to the Graff Hotel. The first two Bake-Offs had been brilliantly organized, fun affairs and had raised a great deal of money between the auctions, entrance tickets, and raffles but they were going one step up for the grand finale. Graff's was the fanciest hotel in town, recently and lovingly restored to mix every modern amenity with old-time class and charm.

The bachelors were being given free range of the top-class kitchens to create their cakes and the products of their labors were to be sold as part of a full afternoon tea to the paying guests. Tickets were priced high and the final presentation would take place in the gorgeous opulent ballroom. Lacey knew that several of the town's wealthiest citizens had been making noises to Jane about making a significant contribution to the appeal and this afternoon was exactly the right time for them to follow through on their promises. And where they led many people might follow.

But Lacey couldn't quite muster up her old enthusiasm. She was pleased for Jane and all the other people who had put so much time and energy into the Bachelor Bake-Off—and of course she was delighted that Harry's House looked like becoming a reality, but every time she thought of seeing Zac, of acting cool and casual, her stomach dropped. Even biscuits and cake and little fancy sandwiches didn't interest her and that was a very bad sign.

It didn't take her long to walk to the stately old hotel, even with her camera bag weighing her down, and she was soon inside and beginning to set up. The last two weeks she had been the only media person there, wearing both her radio and web PR hats, but she rapidly realized that today was a very different story. Several reporters were hanging around reception and at least two TV crews were setting up with wires and large microphones and huge cameras, creating quite the stir.

Lacey patted her own little camera affectionately. It might not have the imposing presence of the professional crews' kits but at least she could operate it on her own. She switched it on and began to double-check the settings, a little shy in this room full of professionals.

"Lacey? Lacey Hathaway? Is that you? I thought I recognized you." A tall woman had broken away from one of the crews and tapped her way smartly across the lobby. She was impressive in a well-cut red suit, her hair twisted into a neat chignon, her makeup impeccable.

"Hi, yes, I'm Lacey." She racked her brains as she held out her hand. Surely she'd remember if she had met this woman before?

"Annabel, Annabel Whyte." The woman introduced herself. "Lacey, I have been loving your webcasts. That's why we're here in fact. We knew our viewers would love Marietta's Bachelor Bake-Off as much as we do. Tell me—" she lowered her voice conspiratorially "—which of those gorgeous men do you think will win? I can't help but notice a certain tension between you and Zac. I absolutely adore your own mini bake-offs and I have to say, I would find it very hard to concentrate with those cheekbones there to distract me. No." as Lacey searched for something to say that wouldn't incriminate her. "You don't have to say a word. The camera never lies and he can't take those dreamy eyes off you either. Delicious."

"Oh... I..." Darn it, so much for cool and collected. She was burning up and so flustered she couldn't get a word out.

"So tell me, Lacey, you live right here in Marietta—what does a bright girl like you do day to day?"

Solid ground. Lacey grabbed the safe topic thankfully. "I run the local radio station, I have the afternoon drive time slot and I'm the station manager as well, plus corporate videos and some online work like the Bake-Off films."

"And you enjoy that?"

"Yes. But I am wondering where to go next." The words had left Lacey's mouth before she was even aware that she was going to utter them; but once they were said the truth of them hit home. At some point, without even noticing it, she had outgrown the cozy world she had hidden away in. She was ready to spread her wings a little. Anticipation shivered through her, warring with fear and excitement. "I love what I've done with the station but I don't think there's enough in Marietta to enable me to grow."

Annabel Whyte's smile widened. "That is really good news. I produce *Meeting Montana* and we are on the lookout for a community reporter. Someone to cover events like this, put a feature together for our Friday evening show, and come into the studio in Billings to chat about it and also release two- or three-minute teaser segments for our online channel every weekday. It could be learning to bake with lovely bachelors like this, covering the new tango classes in Missoula, or spending a whole week at the State Fair. Fun, community-minded but with a heart—just like your online channel."

"That sounds like an amazing opportunity." Lacey's heart was hammering. A job like that would mean statewide travel, staying over in different towns—possibly a night in Billings every week—but she could still have a base in Marietta if she wanted. Although, much as she loved her great-aunts, maybe at twenty-five it was time to move out of Crooked Corner and fend for herself. She should know how to pay her own bills and buy—and cook—her own groceries and when to call a plumber. It was time to grow up.

"I'd love to discuss it with you further." Annabel handed her a business card. "Call me next week and we can arrange for you to come in and have a chat and maybe a screen test. Based on what I've seen I think you would be a perfect fit, Lacey. Think about it."

"I will, thank you so much." Lacey pocketed the card, her blood thumping as she did so.

"Great, I look forward to hearing from you." Annabel turned back to her crew with a last smile at Lacey who stood holding her camera, her knuckles white. This opportunity might not work out but it was a definite sign. Her life needed to be shook up and she was finally going to do it—with or without Zac Malone.

ZAC BREATHED A sigh of relief as he finally pulled up at the Graff Hotel. A delayed flight had meant that his already tight schedule had been far too close to the line. He was supposed to start baking in a little over ten minutes.

Luckily Patty Hathaway had promised to have all his ingredients bought and ready at his workstation, although she had been less than impressed with his choices—in marked contrast to his employees who had been equally suspicious and surprised when Zac had shown up to work bearing three sample homemade cakes. They had been even more surprised when he turned up the next day with five.

It hadn't just been the cakes that had surprised them—it had been that Zac himself had brought them into work. It was clear that although they regarded him as a fair boss (he hoped) and that training, development, benefits, and salary were all good for a still small and new company, Zac himself was seen as aloof and apart from his employees. Certainly not someone who would bring in baked goods to the office. Not someone who would have a coffee and a chat in the kitchen while eating said cake.

Turned out the kitchen was the place to find out more about his employees, not just about their lives outside the office but also about their hopes for their future, the ways they saw their roles developing—and they had some good ideas. Ideas he would never hear locked away in his office or on the road.

He got out of the car, wincing as the cold air hit him. He palmed the car key and strode toward the hotel entrance, aware that adrenaline and anticipation were driving him, that every nerve was humming. Where was she?

There was no time to look for Lacey. The second he set foot inside the hotel he was pounced upon by a pacing Jane and escorted through to the kitchens. He blinked. Surely they weren't going to let a bunch of amateurs loose in these state-of-the-art rooms? Not unsupervised, certainly. A man in gleaming chef whites stood by the wall, arms folded and eyes narrowed as he looked each bachelor over. Zac was all too aware that the jeans and shirt he had thrown on this morning were travel-stained and wrinkled. If only he'd had time to change.

"Patty Hathaway gave me these," Jane said and pressed a bag into his hands. "There's a cloakroom out back with a shower if you're quick. We'll be starting in ten minutes."

Zac thanked Jane and sent a heartfelt message to Patty mentally as he looked inside the bag. Fresh gray wool pants, a short-sleeved blue shirt and a folded towel along with, he was devoutly thankful to see, fresh socks.

It took him just under the ten minutes to shower, change, and slip on the crisply ironed apron, which was *de rigueur* for the Bachelor Bake-Off contestants. He checked his workstation. All his ingredients were there. Some wonderful person had put a mug of fresh, strong coffee on the side but something was still missing. He still hadn't seen Lacey and he had no time to look around.

The judges were gathered at the front of the kitchen, notebooks in hand, and there were—he blinked. Good Lord. How many cameras?—press behind them all intently filming. Zac took a look round at his fellow contestants and suppressed a smile as he clocked granite jaws and focused eyes. His fellow bachelors were ready to get their bakes on. Whereas Zac, he just wanted this over and done with so he could finally see his girl.

And then he did. Lacey was standing behind the crowd of reporters and cameras, a one-woman band, her own camera in her hand. He blinked. Her hair was loosely knotted up, wisps falling down to frame her heart-shaped face and instead of her usual uniform of jeans and a soft fitted sweater she wore a pink and white dotted dress which fell to her knee. It was a very demure dress with an old-fashioned vibe, but it clung to her curves lovingly and she took Zac's breath clean away.

She didn't look in his direction though. Not once.

Zac managed to drag at least half his mind to the work at hand. Thank goodness he'd spent every evening christening the hitherto unused oven in his condo, perfecting his cake. He barely needed to use his scales as he creamed his butter and sugar, added the eggs and sifted the flour, adding copious amounts of cinnamon as he did so. And as he mixed and folded and whisked he watched the brightly colored figure make her way around the room, as she teased, flirted, and laughed with every bachelor there except him.

He beat the mixture a little harder.

Peeling, coring, and slicing the apples took a little more concentration if he didn't want to add his own flesh into the recipe. It would, of course, be at that moment Lacey finally showed up at his workstation.

"Last but not least. Bachelor number eight. Hi, Zac, can you tell me about the cake you're baking for us today?" She sounded completely impersonal, as if they hadn't spent a day skiing together, hadn't shared a house and a kitchen, hadn't gone on one perfect date. He should have been cast down by her apparent disinterest but she was trying too hard not to look at him and the hand holding the camera wasn't quite steady.

Zac suppressed a smile. "Apple and cinnamon with a brown sugar topping."

He glanced up in time to see her eyes lighten. "I love cinnamon."

"I know," he said quietly and watched her swallow. "That's why I chose it. It reminds me of you."

She switched the camera off with unsteady hands, laying it down on the counter. "You didn't leave as much as a note."

"I didn't expect to be gone so long."

"That isn't the point."

"I know and I'm sorry. The truth is I didn't know what to say and so I didn't say anything at all."

"It didn't have to be deep and meaningful. Just a quick acknowledgement I existed would have been nice."

He looked down at the half-peeled apple. "I knew you existed, Lacey. I was aware of your existence every moment I was gone." He looked up again. "I like you in that dress by the way. I'd think it was a shame that you usually hide those gorgeous legs of yours in jeans if the thought of anyone else admiring them wasn't driving me half mad with jealousy."

She flushed. "I don't hide them, and you have no call to be jealous, or right to be either, and actually I don't think you should be mentioning my legs at all."

"It's come as a shock to me to find myself behaving like

such a Neanderthal," he agreed. "The last girl I dated was a fitness guru. She spent her life in yoga pants and a cropped top the better to show off her six pack and I never once batted an eyelid when she was openly ogled in the street. Mind you, neither did she. She would usually just hand out her business cards. Her body was literally her business advertisement and very honed it was too, maybe a little too much so. She was all angles, no soft edges anywhere mentally or physically. Besides, it was never going to work out with someone who thought adding nonfat nondairy yogurt to a kale smoothie the height of decadence. So what I am trying to say is that I'm not the jealous type, not usually. And yet here I am."

He picked up the apple and resumed peeling it, resisting the urge to see how—or if—his words had affected Lacey. She stood speechless for a moment and then picked up her camera and walked away. Zac took a deep breath. Step One complete. He had told her that she was unlike anyone else he knew, that the way he felt was unlike anything he had ever experienced before. Now he just had to hope she would allow him to progress to Step Two and change both of their lives. Forever.

Chapter Seventeen

"LACEY, DEAR, YOU look flushed." Aunt Patty arched an elegant eyebrow as Lacey skidded to a halt at the table her aunts had sponsored for the Bachelor Bake-Off afternoon tea.

"Do I? It was hot in that kitchen," not to mention how fast she had exited said kitchen or the way her whole body had heated up to smoking temperature when Zac had told her, in the calmest, most conversational way ever, that she had brought out his inner Neanderthal. She still wasn't sure if that was a good thing or not but her body had decided to run independently of both her head and her heart, and was reacting in overly enthusiastic acceptance.

He hadn't been all cool and collected though. There had been a moment when he had looked straight at her and the heat in his eyes had almost made her combust on the spot.

"How's dear Zac getting on? His cake isn't looking too boring is it?" Aunt Priscilla asked. She had swapped her trademark sweatshirt for a pretty floral blouse, her vibrant hair scooped back in a chignon. It was a shock to see her usual casual and comfortable aunt so dressed up.

"You look beautiful, Aunt P." Not that she was putting off answering the question. How was Zac getting on? She only wished she knew. "Fine, I think. It's pretty busy in there. It's too early to tell what the cake looks like but he seems to have everything under control."

She smiled as brightly as she could but that only made her aunts stare at her harder. "It looks lovely in here," she added quickly. The table was laid for six with delicate china plates and small silver cutlery. A tiered tray sat in the middle of the table laden with a huge variety of tiny sandwiches.

Lacey slipped into the empty seat and looked around the table. Typically her aunts had decided against wining and dining any clients and instead had invited a few friends to the afternoon tea. Ty, looking as uncomfortable as she would expect a teenager to look at a table where the average age of the other diners was over seventy, sat next to her aunt Patty and his grandfather was seated next to Priscilla. Mrs. Hoffmann was sitting on Patty's other side and next to Lacey, and Lacey turned to the older lady in surprise. She hadn't realized the aunts had invited her. "How lovely to see you here, Mrs. Hoffmann. We need to sort out a date to record your memories. I should have some time now the Bake-Off is nearly over."

"Whenever you can manage, dear. I have nothing but time," Mrs. Hoffmann said. "Although the next few weeks will be busy. The house has sold and the buyer wants a quick sale."

Lacey paused, her arm still stretched out toward the sandwiches. "It sold? Already? I thought the realtor said it could take months for a property like that to sell; that's why she asked for the video." It had been a good video but not that good!

"Take a sandwich, Lacey, and stop blocking the table," Aunt Patty said and Lacey hurriedly scooped up two smoked salmon, two beef, and a cheese sandwich. They were so tiny they were barely a mouthful each. "I was with Mrs. Hoffmann when she got the call and she realized she wasn't quite ready to move into a home yet…"

"All those people," the older lady explained. "I'm used to my own space, you know. To doing things at my pace. But I can't live alone either."

"So she's going to come and live with us." Aunt Priscilla eyed the sandwiches. "Do you think it would be greedy to have just one more? I need to save room for biscuits and cake."

"They're so small you could have ten more and it won't make any difference; that's the joy of afternoon tea." Lacey turned to Mrs. Hoffmann. "You're coming to live in Crooked Corner?" That decided it. She loved her great-aunts and liked Mrs. Hoffmann immensely but she couldn't keep living with two nearly seventy-year-olds and a ninety-year-old in Marietta's very own version of *The Golden Girls*. Especially when at times said almost seventy-year-olds seemed a great deal younger than she did.

"Your Aunty Patty suggested it but of course I said no. I don't want to be a burden and there's no reason for her to take me in. But she was very persistent, said I would have my own rooms, complete privacy, and Carola will still come in to clean and help care for me, although your aunts will kindly prepare my meals. I'll be a paying guest. Of course. That I am quite determined on despite what Patty Hathaway thinks."

"It's what Sam would have wanted, and I want to as well. There's a lot of catching up to do." Aunt Patty smiled affectionately at the older woman and Lacey's breath caught in her throat. There was a world of lives not lived and opportunities missed in that smile.

Aunt Patty was the most glamorous person she knew and, as children, Lacey and her cousin Fliss had pored over seventies magazines to see their aunt modeling a variety of outlandish clothes, her lifestyle the stuff of fantasy. But in the end family ties and affection had brought her home and Lacey knew that although her aunt had enjoyed every moment of her improbably glamorous life, part of her had never left Marietta and the man she had loved and lost.

She searched for something to say. "That's great news. Welcome to Crooked Corner. Which suite of rooms will you be moving into?"

Her aunt looked surprised. "The usual ones we rent out; as soon as Zac leaves we'll have them redecorated and freshened up. I think Mrs. Hoffmann will want her own furniture around her."

"It all seems very sensible." Lacey decided to leave her own news about the possible new job and her decision to move out for another day. She would hate for Mrs. Hoffmann to think that her imminent arrival had anything to do with Lacey's departure. Besides, the job was far from a done deal yet.

Lacey stared down at her plate, her throat thick. She might be cross with Zac for leaving without a word—and crosser that he had come back so nonchalantly cool and full of matter-of-fact compliments she hadn't had time to take away and deconstruct—but she still didn't want to face his imminent final departure. When he left next time that would be that. There would be no coming back, no reason for him to come back. Not unless she gave him one—and soon.

LACEY BARELY TASTED the rest of her sandwiches, biscuits, and the slices of Bake-Off cakes that had been divided between the tables—which was a real shame with red velvet cake, and a pumpkin buttermilk cake amongst the contenders, both favorites of hers. She had decided against staying seated for the whole of the tea; instead she took her camera around the room to interview some of the other diners and get them to critique the cakes for her. Every time Zac's apple cinnamon cake got a compliment she found it hard to maintain her professional composure, his words running through her head again and again: "*That's why I chose it. It reminds me of you.*"

Finally, once plates were pushed away and replete diners were murmuring that they couldn't manage one more crumb, the final judging was announced. Lacey made her way, camera as ever in hand, through to the ballroom filled with excited people and a buzz of expectation.

This was it; this was when they would see if they had enough money for the repairs. If not, then the house would be handed over to a commercial business and Harry's House would be nothing but a dream once again. She crossed her fingers. They had all worked so hard. Surely, surely they would hit their target of twenty-five thousand dollars. Her gaze flitted over to the Sheehan brothers, relaxed and laughing in the corner. Lacey was pretty sure that Troy would be putting up a sizeable donation and Cormac was unlikely to let his brother take all the limelight and would match whatever donation was pledged.

The four judges stood at the front of the room, scorecards in hand. Once again the bakes were being judged on everything from texture to looks to taste. The bachelors were standing to one side, joking with each other now that their ordeal had finally nearly ended. Lacey knew all of them either from prior acquaintance or through her promotional work, but her eyes skated past seven of the men, her gaze locking on the intense dark eyes of Zac Malone, his own gaze focused firmly on her. She shivered. There was a purpose and a heat in his eyes mixed with a tenderness she had not seen in him before.

Lacey barely took in the events of the next hour. To nobody's real surprise town vet Matthew West took first prize, Carolyn Hanson and the niece she had moved back to Marietta to raise both whooping loudly at the result. Carolyn was an accomplished chef and, rumor had it, she and Matthew were doing a great deal more than practicing baking together. Lacey barely knew Carolyn but she was fond of Matthew and it was lovely to see him so happy.

Zac came a respectable joint third and she heard both her aunts give audible sighs of relief as the results were announced. As expected several large donations were pledged during the ceremony and the room erupted into cheers when Jane announced that they had met their target and that they would be able to go ahead with making the repairs necessary to turn the old house into a safe space for the town's teens. Cheers which turned to whoops and congratulations when bachelor Tyler Carter, whose baking skills – or lack of – rivalled Lacey's own – stepped up to make a heartfelt speech, culminating in a marriage proposal to his girlfriend, Stacey Allman. Lacey applauded wholeheartedly as Stacey accepted, the couple's joy palpable as they embraced. Lacey's gaze slid over to Zac's and as her eyes met his her heart thumped so audibly she felt as if it must be heard throughout the room.

The room began to empty but Lacey remained rooted to the spot, immobile, her entire being focused on Zac. He was surrounded, people wanting to thank the bachelors, the press wanting photo ops, but every time she looked over he had a small secret smile just for her. With shaking hands she began to put her camera away, murmuring appropriate responses to the farewells and congratulations as people passed her on their way out.

She straightened just as Zac finally freed himself from the knot of people. His walk toward her was unhurried but full of intent. He didn't speak but took her bag, shouldering it as he slipped an arm around her waist and ushered her from the room. He smelt so good, of cinnamon and sugar, of spice and coffee. He smelt like home.

They stayed silent as they exited the hotel and headed into the parking lot but Zac's arm was still around her waist. He stopped by a gleaming black station wagon and pressed the key to open it. With a quick nervous look Lacey slid into the passenger side. Zac got in beside her and started the engine.

"It's all been going on since you left." She couldn't take the silence anymore. "Mrs. Hoffmann has sold her house already. She doesn't know who, cash buyer who wants a quick sale, but get this: she's going to move in to Crooked Corner. I was amazed when the aunts told me but actually when I think about it, it makes perfect sense. It also made me realize that I probably need to move on. I can't live with my aunts forever—much as I love them. And it's bad enough when I'm in alone with the cat when my aunts are out gallivanting but if it turns out that nonagenarian has a better social life than me I will be utterly crushed. Besides, I spoke to this TV producer today who might have an opening for me. It will mean traveling around Montana and probably spending a couple of days a week in Billings…"

She faltered to a stop aware that, as usual, her tongue was running away with her and that they were on Bramble Lane already, only Zac hadn't pulled up at Crooked Corner; instead he had parked opposite Summer House. She shot him a quick glance but his face was shuttered, only his knuckles white on the steering wheel any sign of interior emotion.

"Take a walk?" he said.

She looked down at her pumps and thin panty hose. "I'm not really dressed…"

"Just over there." He nodded at Summer House and she stared in confusion. "It's okay. I have a key and Mrs. Hoffmann is spending the rest of the afternoon at Crooked Corner."

Lacey nodded mutely and followed him out of the car and across Bramble Lane, up the steps she had walked up just over a week before. The house was as beautiful as she remembered, still in need of life and happiness and more TLC than one person could manage even with an entire team of handymen and yard servicers. "How on earth did you get a key? And why?"

Zac turned and smiled. "I asked. Come on in, it's cold."

It was odd stepping into somebody else's home when they weren't there. Like trespassing. Lacey half expected a security person to jump out and demand they freeze right there. She stood in the hallway and put her hands on her hips. "Zac, what's going on?"

"I bought it."

Her heart began to hammer. "Bought what?"

He gestured around. "This, I bought this."

"You're the cash buyer?" She blinked, trying to process the words. "But how? Why?"

"Because you need to be close to Marietta so I needed a base here. It had to be big enough for me to run my company from here, for half the week at least although I will need to be in San Francisco for a couple of days every week—but if you're flitting around Montana that works out fine. It also needed to be big enough for you to have an editing room and anything else you need. And this house needs a family. Needs love. Needs real-life people to keep the ghosts company, to set them free."

"But... but..." Words were going round and round in her head. Family. Love. "I don't understand. You need a lodger? Is that what you mean?"

Zac winced. "I'm going about this all wrong. I was supposed to do this when we got here." He reached into his pocket and pulled out a small box. Lacey stared at it, her mouth dry. "Zac?"

He stepped close and took her hand. "I know it's only been a few weeks but when I turned up in Marietta I was a different man. I was afraid to stop long enough to put down any roots, afraid to let anyone in, afraid to love. I'm not afraid anymore. I love you, Lacey. I love that you care so much; I love that your family and your community mean so much to you; I love that you give everything, that you do your all. I love how you can talk to several thousand people and make each listener feel special; I love how you are willing to put yourself on the line and don't mind how ridiculous it makes you look…"

"You're talking about the cookies…"

A smile curved his mouth. "I love that when you hear someone is in trouble your first instinct is to help; I love that you're competitive and never give up. I love the way you brighten a room just by being in it; I love listening to you play the piano. You're the most beautiful woman I've ever met—inside and out. I know I don't have a lot to offer. I know I'm stuffy and closed in and don't always have a lot to say. I know I…"

Lacey's heart had swelled so big she thought it might break right out of her. She reached up and laid one hand on his mouth. "You stepped right in to help with a fundraiser that you had no connection with. You saw a boy on the street and knew something was wrong long before his own friends and neighbors did. You made me think about my future and what I need from life. You showed me something was missing, something I was too scared to look for. You make me want to do more, want to be more."

Zac took her hand in his, his gaze on hers. "Can you do more, be more with me, Lacey? Could you help me make this house a home? Fill it with love and laughter and happiness once again? I love you, Lacey Hathaway." He flipped open the box and Lacey swallowed as she looked at the sapphire ring sparkling inside. "Sapphires for your eyes. If you don't like it…"

"I love it."

"Then will you wear it? Will you do me the greatest honor and agree to be my wife? I promise to always be a better man with you by my side. I promise to love you and cherish you always."

Lacey nodded, watching as he slid the ring onto her finger. "Do you promise to let me win at skiing competitions?"

Zac cupped her face, his eyes full of a love Lacey had never imagined could exist, not for her. "No, I can't promise you that, but I do promise to do all the baking in this house."

"In that case, Zac Malone, I will marry you." She leaned into his caress, into his kiss, and as she did so it was as if the house and those who had once lived and loved here gave them their blessing and Lacey knew that after a lifetime of searching she had finally come home.

The End

You'll love the next book in the…

Bachelor Bake-Off series

Available now at your favorite online retailer!

About the Author

An ex au-pair, bookseller, marketing manager and seafront trader, Jessica now works for an environmental charity in York. Married with one daughter, one fluffy dog and two dog-loathing cats she spends her time avoiding housework and can usually be found with her nose in a book. Jessica writes emotional romance with a hint of humour, a splash of sunshine and a great deal of delicious food – and equally delicious heroes.

Thank you for reading

Baking for Keeps

If you enjoyed this book, you can find more from all our great authors at TulePublishing.com, or from your favorite online retailer.

TULE
PUBLISHING

Made in the USA
Columbia, SC
08 August 2021